He wanted the truth, but how could she tell him about that awful night?

"Talk to me, Lydia." The warmth in Matt's voice touched her. She gazed into his eyes and saw something she hadn't seen before—compassion, concern, empathy. "What happened in Atlanta?"

"There...there was a fire." Whether it was the late hour or the haunting memory, the words slipped out before she realized. Her palms grew damp. "I got Tyler outside and went back for Sonny...but there was no hope."

Matt reached out and wrapped his arm around her shoulders. She dropped her head onto his chest and let the tears fall. She cried for her husband who had died, for her son exposed to too much pain and for a way of life that had been introduced to an unending fear.

DEBBY GIUSTI

is a medical technologist who loves working with test tubes and petri dishes almost as much as she loves to write. Growing up as an army brat, Debby met and married her husband—then a captain in the army—at Fort Knox, Kentucky. Together they traveled throughout the world, raised three wonderful army brats of their own and now see the military tradition carried on in their son, who's also in the army. Always busy with church, school and community activities, Debby knew it was time to settle down and write her first book when she and her family moved to Atlanta, Georgia. Despite occasional moments of wanderlust, Debby spends most of her time writing inspirational romantic suspense for Steeple Hill.

Debby wants to hear from her readers. Contact her c/o Steeple Hill, 233 Broadway, Suite 1001, New York, NY 10279. Visit her Web site at www.debbygiusti.com and e-mail her at debby@debbygiusti.com.

NOWHERE TO HIDE
Debby Giusti

Steeple
Hill®

Published by Steeple Hill Books™

STEEPLE HILL BOOKS

Steeple Hill®

ISBN-13: 978-0-373-44239-3
ISBN-10:   0-373-44239-4

NOWHERE TO HIDE

Copyright © 2007 by Deborah W. Giusti

www.SteepleHill.com

Printed in U.S.A.

The Lord is a refuge for the oppressed, a stronghold in times of trouble. Those who know YOUR name will trust in YOU, for YOU, Lord, have never forsaken those who seek YOU.

—*Psalms 9:9–10*

To my wonderful husband, Tony
For your love, support and encouragement.
You've always believed in me. Thank you, honey.

To Elizabeth, Joseph and Mary
God blessed me abundantly with the gift of
each of you. No mother could be more proud
of her children.

To Sharon Yanish, Dianna Love Snell,
Darlene Buchholz and Annie Oortman
Dear friends and outstanding critique partners

To Georgia Romance Writers
Especially Mae Nunn, Jennifer LaBrecque,
Doreen Graham, Anna DeStefano, Rita Herron,
Stephanie Bond, Karen White, Wendy Wax,
Nancy Knight and Carmen Green

To Love Inspired authors
Margaret Daley and Lenora Worth

To my editor, Krista Stroever

ONE

"Not my baby!"

In a split second, Lydia Sloan saw everything unfold—the black Mercedes parked in the deserted school yard, the tinted window partially lowered, her six-year-old son's hesitation before he stepped toward the stranger's car.

Fear shoved her heart into her throat.

She swerved to the curb, clawed at the door of her SUV and leaped into the late-afternoon storm. The wind pulled at her hair and rain slapped against her face as the buzzer on the dashboard blared a warning she'd left her key in the ignition. All she cared about was the alarm going off in her head.

Someone was trying to kidnap her son.

"Tyler!" she screamed as she ran toward him.

Her feet splashed through puddles. Water splattered her legs. She slipped, caught herself, then continued on, desperate to reach her son.

Her lungs burned like fire. If anything happened to Tyler, she would never breathe again. Over and over, she cried his name, but the storm drowned out her words.

Her son moved closer to the Mercedes.

Lydia surged forward, flailing her arms. "Tyler! No! Stay away from the car!"

He was oblivious to the warning.

"God, help me." She cried.

Lightning ripped through the sky. Hit its mark. Thunder exploded behind her.

Tyler jumped at the sound. He turned, saw her and stepped away from the car. The door opened. A hand reached out to grab him. Fingers hooked his book bag.

He jerked free.

"Run, Tyler!"

A moment later, he was in her arms. His small fingers dug into her neck. She hugged him tight, both of them crying as they clung to one another.

The door of the Mercedes slammed shut. The sedan sped out of sight.

Lydia's heart pounded against her chest. Her breath came in ragged gulps as she struggled to control the panic threatening to overpower her. Falling to her knees, she ignored the pouring rain, thinking only about the softness of the body pressed against her. She rubbed her hands over Tyler's shoulders and down his back, wanting to touch every inch of him. She raked her fingers through his wet hair, pulled his head back to stare into his troubled blue eyes and then drew his trembling body even deeper into her embrace.

It had been seven months since her husband's death and she had tried to pretend everything would get better. But it hadn't. The pinpricks of fear that randomly tickled her neck weren't her imagination. The footprints in the mud behind the apartment had been real. Someone had been watching…and waiting.

Why had the police chosen today to reopen the questioning about Sonny's death? They had grilled her for hours until she demanded to be released to pick up her son from school. But her timing was off. Friday-afternoon traffic and she'd almost arrived too late.

Tyler looked at her, his eyes swollen with tears, his blond hair plastered against his round face. "He said he was a friend of Dad's."

Lightning slashed through the sky and thunder rolled across the empty school yard.

"It's okay, honey," she said, hoping her voice belied the terror that had taken hold of her.

A black Mercedes had tried to run Sonny off the road just days before his death. Now, someone driving the same make of car had attempted to grab Tyler. Without a doubt, the person or persons who killed her husband were also after her son.

But why? Because of the evidence Sonny had hidden? By taking Tyler did the murderers think they could get to her? Maybe convince her to turn over the names of the influential people involved in the corruption? Names she didn't have. Information she'd never seen.

If only Sonny hadn't been so secretive. So deceptive.

Lydia pulled in a deep breath as a surge of determination coursed through her veins. She had to protect her son. More than anything, she and Tyler needed a safe haven where they could hide—at least for a few days.

Only one place came to mind.

"Tyler, we're going to Sanctuary Island."

The night surrounded Lydia, dark as pitch and sinister as the man who had tried to grab her son earlier in the day. Wind howled through the tall Georgia pines and mixed with the roar of angry surf crashing upon the beach as Lydia steered her vehicle down the unlit path.

A flash of lightning momentarily illuminated the foreboding structure before her. Safe haven? The island home looked about as welcoming as a witch's den with its deep recesses and dark shadows.

She braked the SUV to a stop and pushed open the driver's door. Fog seeped from the sodden ground as she stepped into the damp night. The smell of musky earth and sea brine hung heavy in the air. Beside the house, a giant live oak stood guard. Draped in Spanish moss, its branches twisted skyward into oblivion.

"Stay in the car, Tyler."

A pot of geraniums sat on the porch right where she'd been told. She shoved the heavy clay container aside. Groping with her hand across the wet brick, she found the key and folded scrap of paper before she returned to the circle of light falling from the open car door.

Tyler watched her, his brow wrinkled with more worry than a little boy should ever have to carry. Too much had happened too fast. After all these months of trying to get their lives back together, in one afternoon everything had fallen apart. Lydia would cry if she weren't so tired. And scared.

Clutching the key, she unfolded the soggy paper Katherine had promised to leave with the security code and bent toward the light. Lydia's stomach twisted into a hard knot. The rain had blurred the ink into an unreadable smudge. A rumble of thunder rolled through the night as if the storm was gathering strength for another onslaught.

"Come on, Tyler. Let's get inside."

The boy slid across the seat and dropped his feet onto the wet pavement. "I'm afraid."

Lydia rubbed her hand across her son's slender shoulders. She needed to be strong for Tyler.

"It's okay, honey. Everything's going to be fine."

The wind died momentarily, but the sound of the ocean crashing on the shoreline continued. Lydia shivered as she stuck the key in the lock, turned it counterclockwise then pushed the door open. Darkness greeted her.

One step at a time, she told herself, pulling in a deep breath and moving her hand across the wall.

She found the light switch, flipped it on, but the darkness remained.

"The storm probably knocked out the power," she said, hearing a glimmer of hope in her voice. Without electricity, the security alarm wouldn't work—she turned her head, spied the row of lights glowing from the keypad on the far wall—unless the system was powered by a backup battery source. A high-pitched hum signaled the alarm was engaged, security had been breached. Thirty seconds later, a deafening screech blasted through the night.

Tyler covered his ears to block out the blare. Lydia still held the crumpled paper. If only the rain hadn't smeared the ink.

She tried to recall important dates—birthdays, anniversaries, anything that might be the correct sequence of numbers. She tapped in four digits, pushed enter then waited for the heinous noise to still.

Frantically, she tried another combination. Then another.

A lump clogged Lydia's throat as she blinked back tears that threatened to spill down her cheeks. She wouldn't let Tyler see her cry.

A phone rang, the sound barely audible over the roar of the alarm. She moved into the kitchen, worked her hand across the granite countertop, knocked the phone off the receiver, then somehow managed to grab it before it fell to the ground.

"This is Sanctuary Alarm Service," a woman's voice drawled across the line.

Lydia clutched the edge of the kitchen counter as her body slumped with relief. "I'm glad you called. The alarm—"

"Password, please."

"I'm afraid I… You see, my son and I—"

"Password?"

"I'm sorry—"

The phone clicked dead. Lydia dropped it back onto the receiver as Tyler moved closer.

"It's gonna be okay, Mom."

She wrapped her arms around her son. As far as she was concerned, things couldn't get much worse.

Then a beam of light sliced through the darkness as someone pushed the front door open.

TWO

Matt Lawson peered into the darkness, saw movement and aimed his gun. "Hold it right there." He raised the flashlight in his left hand. The arc of light broke through the darkness. "Sanctuary Security. Step toward me. Hands in the air."

No reaction.

"Now, buddy!"

A woman moved from the shadows. Slender. Five foot six. Shoulder-length blond hair. A child peered around the counter. She shoved him protectively behind her.

"What's going on, ma'am?"

Lightning illuminated the spacious kitchen. Two seconds later, a clap of thunder confirmed a nearby hit.

Why in the world would a woman and child break into one of the prestigious homes on Sanctuary Island? The woman certainly didn't look as if she belonged in the upscale community. Wrinkled clothes. Hair hanging limp around her oval face. She reminded him of a stray cat, needing to be fed.

Matt shook his head ever so slightly. The past year working security on the island must have skewed his common sense. He'd seen plenty of female perpetrators on the streets of Miami.

Didn't matter how pathetic the woman standing before him looked, he'd still have to take her back to the office, question her and, if need be, call in the mainland sheriff's office.

No reason why this scared wisp of a thing couldn't be up to no good in coastal Georgia.

"What's your name, ma'am?"

"Who are *you?*" she demanded, finally finding her voice.

"Chief Lawson, island security."

She shifted her weight and stuck her chin in the air. A defiant gesture that didn't match the glint of fear flashing from her eyes.

"Then show me some identification," she insisted.

The alarm continued to shriek a warning. Letting out a frustrated breath, Matt tucked the flashlight under his arm, pulled his radio from his belt and punched in a number, never taking his eyes off the woman.

"Eunice, this is Matt. I'm over at 50 Cove Road. Turn off the alarm."

The house fell silent.

He traded the radio for his badge.

She stepped closer, read the information, then glanced up at him as if comparing his face to the photo.

"Now what's your name?" he repeated.

"It's Lydia…Lydia Sloan. And I don't appreciate you barging in and scaring me half to death."

Her assertive attempt fell flat. She looked tired and more than a bit confused.

Lowering his voice, he repeated, "You need to tell me what you're doing here."

She crossed her arms over her chest and stared back at him, as if weighing her options.

"Katherine O'Connor invited us," she finally said.

Matt shook his head. "Why would—"

"She said my son and I could stay while she's on a trip to Ireland," the woman quickly added, then blinked.

Innocent eyes. He thought he could read people. Hard to believe Ms. O'Connor would have house-guests when she was out of the country.

He looked at the boy, small, slender like his mom, with her blue eyes and blond hair. The kid could play a cherub in a Christmas play and steal the show.

A look of determination washed across the boy's face. "Don't you arrest my mom."

The last thing he wanted was to scare a child. "Look, son—"

"I'm not your son," the boy shot back.

The woman wrapped her arm around the boy's shoulders. "Tyler, please."

Matt raised his gaze. The woman watched him, eyes filled with suspicion, face drawn tight with worry.

"How'd you get inside the house, ma'am?"

"Katherine left a key on the porch."

He chuckled under his breath. "Kind of makes my job a little tougher when the residents leave a welcome mat out for anyone who happens along."

"I beg your pardon?" Lydia's body stiffened. "As I said, Tyler and I were invited here."

"But Ms. O'Connor turned on the alarm? Now, that makes about as much sense as—"

"I can explain." The woman held out a crumpled wad of paper. "She left the code for me. The rain smeared the ink."

He took the paper from her hand, unfolded it and aimed the flashlight. Peacock-blue ink. The same distinctive color Ms. O'Connor had used when she'd completed the out-of-town paperwork requesting additional surveillance of her home. Of course, she hadn't mentioned any houseguests.

"Funny, she could have given you the code over the phone," he said.

Lydia shrugged. "I didn't have paper to write on. Katherine said she'd leave it under the plant. We never expected the rain."

The woman appeared to be telling the truth. But better to play it safe. A number of homes on the mainland had been burglarized recently. Wouldn't take much for trouble to make its way to the island.

"Let's take a tour of the house. You lead the way, ma'am."

She hesitated. "Is this necessary?"

"'Fraid so. I need to make sure no one else is hanging around."

"Well, of all the—"

"Call it what you like, ma'am. Let's get started."

She sighed, but nodded for the boy to walk with her, then kept her hand on his shoulder as if to ensure he wouldn't stray from her side. Matt stepped around the counter and worked his flashlight over the adjoining great room.

A painting hung on the wall, Christ in a fishing boat with the disciples, calming the Sea of Galilee.

Matt glanced outside. The cloud cover broke momentarily. The moon peeked through the large Palladian windows that stretched across the back of the house. A ribbon of moonlight glowed along the beach and the ocean beyond. Eight-foot waves. Too bad the Good Lord hadn't calmed the sea tonight.

"Keep moving," Matt said, his eyes probing the shadowed corners of the room, behind the double sofas and the Queen Anne chairs.

The master bedroom. Adjoining bath with the largest tub he had ever seen. Walk-in closet.

Everything in place, neat as a pin. No sign of forced entry or other presence. Three guest bedrooms, two baths. A small office, undisturbed.

The tension in his neck eased as he let out a deep breath. "Looks like you two are the only ones I have to worry about tonight."

The woman whirled around to face him. A streak of moonlight fell upon her face. She was pretty, or would be if her lips weren't drawn tight with resolve. Right now, she looked like a mare ready to trample anyone or anything that ventured too near her new-born colt.

"Calm down, lady," Matt said. "No use getting riled up."

"Look, Mister—"

"Matt," he reminded her. "Matt Lawson."

"I don't appreciate Sanctuary Island's welcoming committee."

Spunky, he'd give her that much. "Just doing my job."

The woman's anger dissipated ever so slightly. "Katherine is my husband's aunt."

Family? "Any way you can prove that? Photos maybe?"

She shook her head. "I don't know where they'd be. Katherine moved here about eight months ago. We've never visited before."

We? "You and your husband?"

She shook her head. "He…" She cleared her throat, pursed her lips, then swallowed. When she spoke, the words came out a whisper.

"My husband died a few months ago."

Not what he expected. He looked at the boy. Either the kid was Academy Award material or the story was legit.

"How'd you get past the gate guard?" Matt asked.

She hesitated as if the question had caught her by surprise. "I didn't see a gate."

"At the turnoff from the Bay Road?"

She shook her head. "The storm…it was raining."

"There's only one way in." Who had gate duty tonight? He tried to think. Sam Snyder. Of all the luck. Sam should have retired years ago. The old guy had probably fallen asleep in the guardhouse. But why had he left the gate open?

Once again, Matt yanked the radio off his belt, punched in a number and put the receiver to his ear. "Eunice, contact Jason. See if he can run by the guardhouse, check on Sam. And look up Ms. O'Connor's paperwork. As I recall, she went to Ireland to help her sister-in-law."

He glanced out the window while Eunice searched for the file.

"Here it is, Chief. Orlando to Dublin. Nonstop." The dispatcher told him the arrival time.

"Any mention of a houseguest?"

"Not a word."

"Contact the airport in Dublin. Leave instructions for her to call me ASAP."

"Will do."

He parked the radio back on his belt. Lydia Sloan's story was probably legit, but Matt needed confirmation from Ms. O'Connor before he allowed the woman and her son access to the home.

Too bad Ms. O'Connor hadn't noted the arrival of guests on the paperwork. Would have made it so much easier.

"Okay, ma'am. We'll go over to my office and wait till we hear from Ms. O'Connor."

She bit her lip, blinked and looked like a scared

rabbit in a trap. "I...I don't understand why that's necessary."

"Yes, ma'am. I hear you. But it's policy here on the island." He stretched out a hand. "Now, if you'll pass me the key, we'll lock this place up tight as a drum so no one else decides to visit."

"It's late." She looked at her son, then back at Matt. "We've been on the road for a long time. It's past his bedtime."

He nodded. "I understand. But we'll head to my office, in spite of the hour. Wait for that phone call."

The woman stooped down to the boy's level. She tried to smile, made her voice sound almost light-hearted. "Okay, Tyler, we have to go with the security man."

"Can I get my Action-Pac?"

She glanced up at Matt. "It's a computerized game. It should be in the front seat of my SUV."

Matt nodded. "That'll be all right."

He locked the door as they left and tried it once to ensure it held tight. Moonlight cascaded down the driveway. Maybe the storm had finally passed.

Tyler climbed into the SUV and retrieved a small electronic toy.

"Bring something to read," Lydia said. "We may have to wait awhile."

A school backpack lay on the seat. Tyler rummaged through it, then pulled out a book.

Matt watched the boy.

Other than the schoolbag, the car sat empty.

Why would a woman and her son, who claimed to be houseguests, arrive late at night with only the clothes on their backs?

Matt shook his head. It was going to be a long night.

Lydia sat next to Tyler in the front seat of the security chief's pickup. The road stretched before them dark and desolate. The truck's headlights cut a path through the night, exposing a roadway strewn with twigs and branches the storm had ripped from the tall pine trees.

Maybe coming to Sanctuary had been a mistake. She'd made too many already. Sonny, their marriage, believing God could turn bad times good....

Nothing had worked out the way she planned. She was too naive. Stupid, Sonny would have called it. But the fact was, she had trusted her husband. And she'd been hurt because of it. Worse than that, Tyler had been hurt.

Seeing her son's pain was a hundred times worse than enduring it herself. No child should have to worry about someone grabbing him in the school parking lot or whether his mother would be the next to die.

She wrapped her arm around her son, pulled him close, then allowed herself to glance at the security man. The glow from the dashboard lights played across his long legs and muscular body.

She hoped to find a bit of softness in his angular face, but all she saw was determination. The guy was one hundred percent business with deep-set eyes that bore into her like a hot poker whenever he looked her way.

As if aware of her perusal, he turned his head toward her. "You okay?"

His voice rang warm with concern. His eyes seemed softer this time. Or maybe she imagined the change.

"I can turn on a little heat if you're cold," he said.

She shook her head and found her voice. "I'm fine."

He studied her for a heartbeat, then returned his attention to the road.

Thick vegetation bordered the pavement. If Katherine had neighbors, Lydia would be hard-pressed to find them. "It's so isolated here," she said, then wished she hadn't given voice to the thought.

"Private's the word we prefer. Five-acre lots with plenty of green space. Walk along the beach and you'll see the homes, each one an architect's delight."

She thought about the drive from Atlanta, the final stretch along the narrow two-lane roads. "But so far from civilization."

"That's the attraction. Folks here like their anonymity. No one bothers them this far off the beaten path. There's a little town on the mainland about thirty minutes west of here. It's got a few shops and restaurants."

"Sounds like a metropolis." She almost laughed. "How'd you end up in Sanctuary?"

Why had she asked that question? She didn't want to get personal.

He tilted his head and glanced out the driver's window. "Kind of fell into it," was all he volunteered.

Ten minutes later, they walked into his office. A

large, mahogany desk took up the major portion of the room. A bookcase stood behind the leather swivel chair, open Bible on the shelf.

The chief appeared to be neat, organized, perhaps a bit on the obsessive-compulsive side with everything in its place, corners squared, not even a speck of dust. A photo of a young boy, a year or two older than Tyler, hung on the wall next to a row of plaques and commendation awards.

Matt motioned for them to sit on the couch in the corner of the room. He settled into the desk chair and pulled a tablet and pen from a drawer, then turned to face them.

"You've got a Fulton County license plate. Still living in Atlanta?"

She nodded.

"Address?"

"Am I being interrogated?" She tried to sound assertive, hoping he didn't recognize the nervous edge to her voice. "Katherine will confirm that Tyler and I are invited guests."

He stared back at her for a moment, glanced at Tyler sitting next to her, then nodded. "Okay. We'll wait till she calls."

"Thank you."

"Well…" He looked around the office. "I think I'll catch up on some paperwork."

Tyler turned on his Action-Pac and flicked his fingers over the buttons that moved the animated figures across the screen.

"Why don't I read you a story?" Lydia asked.

"Ah, Mom. I'm almost finished with this A.P. game disc."

The security chief booted up his computer. "That the new Action-Pac line?"

Tyler nodded.

"Friend of mine says it's the hottest stuff on the market. Vic calls himself a techno junkie with an A.P. addiction." Matt shook his head and chuckled. "T-shirts, coffee mugs, screen savers. Anything made with the A.P. logo and he's got it."

"Cool. My dad bought me my Action-Pac." Tyler's voice was filled with pride.

Sonny had never been one to buy expensive gifts, but he'd given the game to Tyler the night he died. Since then, her son hadn't let it out of his sight.

As the security chief began to type, Lydia whispered into Tyler's ear. "Honey, remember when I checked the A.P. game discs Dad gave you?"

"Yeah. You said you had to look at them before I did."

"That's right. You gave me *all* the discs, didn't you?"

Tyler shrugged. "I think so. Why, Mom?"

Why? Because she wondered whether her computer-whiz husband had hidden evidence on one of the discs, evidence to protect himself before he walked away from the corruption.

Tyler leaned back against her. She wrapped her arm around him, enjoying the warmth of his body nestled close. Her taut muscles began to relax.

Maybe coming to Sanctuary would provide a few days of reprieve, which she desperately needed. She had worked so hard these last months to find out what had happened to Sonny. The fire hadn't been an accident. Someone had wanted him dead. But who and why? The police? Someone at the club?

She had asked God to help her learn the truth. So far, He'd ignored her request.

The security chief—

What was his name?

She glanced at a plaque on the wall. Matt Lawson, that was it.

Her eyes strayed to a certificate with The City of Miami Police Department scripted in gold. "In grateful appreciation for services rendered."

A former cop. No wonder Mr. Lawson seemed unsympathetic to her situation. Of course, in his defense she hadn't given him enough information to realize why she was so cautious. Maybe he'd be more understanding if he knew the truth.

Not that she was willing to explain anything.

Slowly, the tension that had held her tight for so long eased. Her eyes grew heavy. Her mind began to drift....

A phone rang. She jerked awake with a start. Tyler was sound asleep, slumped in her arms. Her watch read 2:00 a.m.

Matt said something into the phone, then smiled in her direction.

"That's good to hear, Ms. O'Connor. Yes, she and

her son arrived a few hours ago. There was a problem with the security alarm." He motioned for Lydia.

Katherine's voice sounded tired when Lydia put the phone to her ear.

"Sorry about the alarm," Katherine said. "I probably should have canceled my trip."

"And I told you I wouldn't hear of it. Your sister-in-law's counting on you," Lydia hastened to reply.

"Hip replacement at age eighty-two. She'll need more than my help. I told Matt you were to be given every courtesy. Don't forget, there are spare clothes in the guest room and a charge card in the desk drawer."

"That's not necessary," Lydia said.

"Buy Tyler a few things for me and don't be stubborn. You don't want anyone to trace your credit card. Order anything you need from The Country Store. It's about fifteen miles west of the island. And there's a small grocery not far from the house. We can settle up when I return, if you insist."

"I can't thank you enough."

"You helped me when Patrick died. Fact is grief probably would have killed me if you hadn't forced me to work through my misery. I know what desperate feels like."

Lydia blinked back tears of appreciation.

"Plus, I never thought Sonny was good enough for you, but that's beside the point. The only thing of value he ever did was tell me about Sanctuary. Eight months ago when Atlanta held too many memories, the ocean was just what I needed. Maybe it'll help you, as well. Now, let me give you the security code before I forget."

Lydia wrote the numbers on a scrap of paper.

"Tell Matt he owes you a dinner for all the trouble he's caused."

"No harm done," Lydia said.

"The man's got a good heart, it's just that his head gets in the way sometimes. And don't listen to the island gossip. He's more than paid for his sins. Listen, I've got to go, the limousine's ready to leave for the hotel. I'm praying for you, Lydia. Call you in a day or two."

Lydia hung up the phone. Unlike her own lukewarm attitude toward the Almighty, Katherine seemed on fire with the love of the Lord. Maybe He'd listen to *her* prayers.

Matt stood and walked around his desk as Lydia returned to the couch. "The electricity should be on by now. I'll drive you and Tyler back to the house."

She nudged her sleeping child. "Wake up, honey."

Tyler rubbed his eyes. "I'm thirsty, Mom."

Matt dug into his pocket, pulled out some change and pointed to a side door. "There's a soda machine down that hall. Connects with the Community Center." He dropped the coins in Tyler's outstretched hand.

"Thank you," Lydia said, following Tyler through the doorway.

Tyler ran to the machine. "Can I get a cola?"

"An orange drink or lemon-lime. You decide."

While Tyler studied the selection, Lydia glanced

at a glass-covered bulletin board filled with photographs that hung on the wall.

Island Life, a sign read, thumbtacked to the center of the grouping on the wall. Joel Cowan, photographer.

Although she and Sonny had never been to Sanctuary, the four-by-six glossies seemed to capture the casual lifestyle of coastal living. A few photos showed pleasure crafts docked at a marina. Others were of fishermen hauling in their catch and men and woman enjoying the sun and the surf.

Wonder if she'd find Katherine's face in the collage.

One photo caught her eye. A group of seagulls hovered in midflight, snagging morsels of bread thrown aloft by someone out of camera range.

She smiled at the birds' frenzy as they vied for food. Two figures stood in the background of the photo. One man watched the gulls while the other—his face cropped off the picture—draped his arm around the first man's shoulder.

Tyler inserted the coins into the slot. A can dropped to the bottom of the machine. "I got an orange soda." He ran back to where she stood and popped the top.

The phone rang in the security chief's office. Lydia glanced through the open door. "Busy place," she muttered watching as Matt picked up the receiver.

"Lawson." He paused for a moment. "Why'd you leave the gatehouse, Sam?"

The chief's body tensed. "How bad is it?"

Matt nodded. "I'll contact the mainland sheriff."

Tyler took a long sip of the cold drink, then skipped toward the office, can in hand. "Come on, Mom. Time to go to Aunt Katherine's."

"Be there in a second."

Lydia glanced back at the bulletin board. Something seemed familiar. She bent closer, squinted her eyes. The man in the photo—

"Sonny?"

Lydia sucked in a lungful of air. Her husband was the man in the photo.

But Sonny never had wanted to visit Sanctuary with his wife and son. Whenever Katherine invited them to visit, he would adamantly refuse, claiming he couldn't spare the time.

Yet, his face had been captured in vivid color next to a sign that read, Help Keep Sanctuary Island Clean.

A picture might be worth a thousand words, but Lydia was speechless. Another lie. Another deception. There had been so many.

She shook her head and thought for a moment. Maybe the photo could be the clue she desperately needed.

If she found out what her husband had been doing on the island, she might find information that would lead her to the men in Atlanta who had killed Sonny.

The men who were now after her son.

THREE

"That wraps it up." Wayne Turner, the mainland sheriff, midforties and balding, watched as the emergency road crew positioned the last of the fluorescent pylons to warn motorists traveling the narrow two-lane Bay Road. On each side of the pavement, water slapped against the stone embankment.

Wayne turned to Matt and stretched out his hand. "What a night. Flash floods and another home broken into on the mainland."

Matt returned the handshake. "Kind of spoils the peace and quiet we like here in coastal Georgia."

"So far, the break-ins have stayed in the dock area. I'll pull in a few of our more colorful locals for a little heart-to-heart. Might get lucky."

The sheriff slapped Matt's back, then paused for a moment. "Heard you're leaving."

Matt nodded. "Soon as the Island Association finds a replacement."

"Big shoes to fill."

"Thanks, Wayne."

The sheriff waved his hand in the air and lumbered off to his squad car just as Jason Everett stepped forward. Tall and lanky, the twenty-two-year-old was the youngest member of the security team.

"How's the embankment holding up?" Matt asked.

"Water's high, but the northern wall's still solid. Southern side's a piece a—"

Matt raised a reproachful eyebrow at his outspoken assistant.

"Washed out with the storm is what I was going to say," Jason hastily added.

Matt glanced at his watch. "Don't you have an 8:00 a.m. class?"

"I can skip."

"Not today, Jas. I told you when I hired you, part-time until you get your degree. You've been on the clock for more than fifteen hours. Better head over to the mainland and clean up. I wouldn't want your professor complaining you smelled up his classroom."

Grinning, Jason started to walk toward his pickup. "Heard you had a lady friend in the office last night," he called over his shoulder.

"Eunice talks too much. A houseguest of Ms. O'Connor's had a little problem with the security alarm."

"Right." The kid exaggerated a nod.

"Jason, go home. Clean up. Get to class."

The young guard wiped the smirk from his face but his eyes twinkled with mischief. He raised his right hand to his forehead in a salute. "Yes, sir." Dutifully, he climbed into his pickup and headed toward the mainland.

Matt watched the truck disappear from sight. The kid had the makings of a good cop, just so long as his enthusiasm didn't get the best of him.

Keep him safe, Lord.

The first hint of dawn glowed on the horizon. Overhead, a few stars twinkled, like fireflies on a hot, summer night.

Father, only You know what today will hold. Help me do my job to the best of my ability. Aid me in every endeavor. And forgive me my transgressions.

Lowering his eyes, he stepped toward his truck.

Fair skies and sunshine, the weather reporter had said. A perfect day, except for all that had happened in the last few hours—a woman and child arrived in Sanctuary with only the clothes on their backs and a storm nearly wiped out the island's only connection with the mainland.

Traveling without luggage screamed of running from something. Ms. O'Connor had vouched for her houseguests, yet instinct told Matt that Lydia Sloan's story didn't add up one hundred percent. She was someone to be watched.

Not that he had time to play private investigator. He had reports to file and damage from the storm to assess. He climbed into his truck, pulled onto the pavement and turned left at the next intersection.

So why was he heading north on Cove Road?

Because he couldn't get the woman's vulnerable look out of his head.

And the boy? A couple of years younger but Tyler reminded him of Enrico.

Matt pushed the memory aside and focused on the road ahead. At the turnoff to Katherine's house, Matt lowered his headlights, shoved the gear into neutral and coasted into the driveway.

Lydia's SUV sat near the house exactly where it had been parked earlier. Light filtered through the curtains.

Either the woman didn't like the dark or she was having trouble sleeping.

What's your secret, lady?

Matt stared at the house for a long time, then shifted into reverse and backed onto the main road.

Doubtful she'd be going anywhere soon, especially with a tired little boy in tow. He'd let her rest a few hours, but he'd be back. One way or another, he'd find out what had brought her to Sanctuary.

What did he want?

Lydia peered around the curtain and watched the security chief's pickup disappear.

Tyler lay sleeping in the guest bedroom, but she was too wired to do anything but pace. She had checked the doors and windows more times than she could count to ensure they were locked, and although her body needed rest, her mind kept thinking back on all that had happened over the last seven months— the fire, her husband's death, the attempt to kidnap

Tyler. So much had occurred in such a short period of time. None of it good.

She had hoped Sanctuary would offer just that. Now she wasn't so sure. Maybe her eyes had played tricks on her, but the man in the photo could have been Sonny's twin. If only she could talk to the photographer. Maybe he'd remember when he'd taken the picture. Hopefully he'd be easier to deal with than the security chief who took his job way too seriously.

Lydia rubbed her neck. She wanted a chance to catch her breath and get their lives back to normal. When Katherine came home, Lydia would ask her to watch Tyler while she returned to Atlanta and continued the search for her husband's killer.

Lydia glanced at the clock.

Six in the morning.

The Men's Club in Atlanta closed at three. More precisely, it was *supposed* to close. Since Sonny's death, she'd learned the back room activities lasted until dawn and catered to high rollers with money to pay for extra services and live entertainment.

Ruby Pace worked the front lounge. By now, she'd be home in the midtown condo she shared with her mother and handicapped sister, enjoying some quiet time to herself before the other two women rose at seven.

Lydia picked up the phone and tapped in the Atlanta number.

"Yeah." Ruby answered on the third ring, a tired and angry edge to her voice.

"It's Lydia. Can you talk?"

The voice softened. "Mama and Charise are sleeping. Where you been? I called your apartment."

"We left Atlanta."

"Why?"

"Someone tried to grab Tyler."

Ruby cursed. "They're trying to get to you 'cause of that evidence that Sonny hid. The Club hired him to run their Web site. They never expected him to poke his nose around where it didn't belong."

"The police still think I started the fire."

"You tell 'em anything?" Ruby asked.

"Just that there's more going on at the Men's Club than meets the eye."

"They didn't buy it, did they?"

"Didn't want to buy it is more like it," Lydia said.

"Just like Sonny told you. Enough money going under the table, no one has a problem with the police. Real convenient for the cops to look the other way when their bank accounts are gettin' fat."

"What about those back room files?"

"Girl, they're locked up tight. Give me a little time. The doorman I told you about says he wants out, just like me." She paused. "I'm trying to work a deal. He watches the door while I check the files."

"Call me."

"No way, honey. I don't even want to know where you be hiding. That way Ruby can't tell the man what she don't know."

Lydia shivered, thinking of what would happen to

Ruby if anyone at the club discovered she was talking to Sonny's wife.

"I'm sorry I got you involved," Lydia said.

"My choice. That night you came snooping around the club, I knew you was out of your element. You got nerve, girlfriend. I like that. Plus, I want a new start. I've had enough of this life. Want to move my Mama and Charise away from the city. Get us a little country place."

"Be careful."

"You know I will. By the way, that reporter was back."

"Trish Delaney? What'd she want?"

"Information, just like you. Only she got the cold shoulder and an escort to the door. Maybe you should call her."

"I…I'm not sure, Ruby."

"Whatever. Talk to me in about a week. I might have something by then."

Lydia hung up. Hopefully, Ruby would find evidence to prove the club was a front for something illegal. If she was lucky, information about Sonny's death might surface, as well.

Whatever Sonny had been involved in now threatened Tyler's life. Much as it terrified her to hunt Sonny's killer, she'd do anything to protect her child.

Lydia pulled down the covers and crawled into bed. Just so Ruby didn't get hurt in the process.

Reaching to turn off the bedside lamp, Lydia noticed a small cross-stitch sampler perched near the clock.

Jesus, I Trust In You, was stitched in tiny *X*s across the fabric.

"If only I could," she mumbled as she turned off the light.

The insistent ring of the doorbell woke her. She opened her eyes and squinted against the daylight streaming through the curtains. Her head felt packed with cotton wool. Too little sleep, most of it plagued with dreams of raging infernos, had taken its toll.

Glancing at the bedside clock, she bolted to a sitting position. Half-past eleven. She had slept far longer than she wanted. Not that she felt rested. Anything but.

She yanked the closet door open and pulled out the blouse and skirt she'd worn the night before. Slipping them on, she made her way barefoot toward the living room.

Tyler stood in the doorway of the guest room, dressed in the G.I. Joe briefs and T-shirt he'd slept in. He rubbed his eyes.

"Who's at the door?" he asked between yawns.

"That's exactly what I'm going to find out." She strode past him, working to control the fear prickling her spine. Surely, no one from Atlanta could have tracked them down in the short time they'd been on the island. Maybe that nosy security chief wanted more information.

Stretching on tiptoe, she peered through the door's tiny peephole. The distorted face of a high schooler, probably sixteen or seventeen, filled the glass circle.

Mustering her sternest voice, she demanded, "Who's there?"

"James, from The Country Store. Ms. O'Connor called in a delivery long-distance. Said I was to get everything here by eleven. The storm washed out one of the roads. Had to take a detour."

Lydia unlocked the door, inched it open and glanced first at The Country Store scripted on the truck's side panel and then at the same logo stitched on the youth's polo. She let out a sigh of relief and opened the door wider.

The kid nodded toward the large cardboard box in his arms. "Ms. O'Connor said to send over everything a boy age six might need. I've got a box filled with ladies' things and another one with odds and ends in the truck."

He dropped the first box inside the door and scrambled down the steps to the delivery truck, where he grabbed two more boxes and deposited them one on top of the other in the entryway.

Lydia reached for her purse. "How much do I owe you?"

"Ms. O'Connor took care of it, ma'am." He climbed into his truck and waved as he backed out of the driveway.

Before Lydia could close the door, a second van pulled up to the house and an equally enthusiastic teen bounded toward the porch, carrying two large grocery bags.

"Harry's Market. More groceries in the truck."

Resigning herself to accepting Katherine's generosity, Lydia pointed the boy in the direction of the kitchen and watched as he hauled the bags into the house.

"Be happy to unpack the groceries, if you need help." He placed the last sack on the counter.

"Thanks, that's not necessary." Lydia dug in her handbag and pulled out a few dollar bills.

The teen walked back to where she stood by the door and accepted the tip.

Shoving the money into his pocket, he said, "You're from Fulton County. Atlanta, right?"

She nodded. "That's right."

"Saw license plates just like yours this morning." The kid shook his head. "Stupid Mercedes almost ran me off the road."

The hair rose on the back of Lydia's neck. "What…what color?"

"Black."

She stiffened. Not the car from Atlanta?

"Probably tourists in a hurry to get to the beach," a voice said behind her. Lydia turned to see Matt Lawson leaning against the front porch railing.

"Morning, ma'am." He pulled the baseball cap with the Sanctuary logo off his head and wrapped a tight smile around his broad face. From the looks of his rumpled khaki pants and navy polo, he, too, appeared to be wearing the same clothes he'd worn the night before.

Lydia noticed the creases at the corner of his eyes,

more pronounced in the light of day. Although clean shaven, his face was drawn with fatigue. No doubt the chief had not enjoyed the luxury of even a few hours of sleep.

"Hey, Mr. Lawson." The delivery boy acknowledged Matt with a nod. "Heard there was another break-in last night on the mainland."

"I'm sure Sheriff Turner's on top of it, Blake."

"Harry said no one local would do such a thing." The teen turned toward the delivery van. "'Probably dock riffraff, pure and simple.' That's what Harry said."

"We'll let the sheriff handle the case, Blake."

The kid opened the driver's door, then glanced back, a chagrined expression on his face. "Yes, sir."

"He'll let us know when he uncovers something. 'Till then, you keep your mind on your business and not the sheriff's. Hear me? And I want to see you at church tomorrow."

"I'll be there." Blake climbed into the van, started the engine and pulled out of the drive.

Lydia stood in the open doorway and glanced down at her bare feet. Her cheeks warmed with a mixture of annoyance and embarrassment. Once again, the chief had caught her by surprise.

Why did that bother her?

Probably because she was out of her element and scared to death every time she thought of how close her son had come to being kidnapped—by someone in a black Mercedes. The delivery boy had seen the same *make* of car, not the same *car*.

Get a grip, Lydia.

She looked up to find the security chief staring at her.

"More questions, Mr. Lawson?" Her voice carried more than a hint of disapproval. "I suppose Katherine called you this morning. She probably told you to make amends."

He shook his head. "Haven't heard from Ms. O'Connor today. And I was doing my job last night."

"Of course you were." She let out a deep breath, fatigue skewing her good judgment. She was taking out her frustration with Atlanta's dirty cops on a guy who managed security systems and island gate guards.

"Look, I'm sorry. It was a long night, and I doubt either of us got much sleep. Why don't we start over?" She stuck out her right hand. "Lydia Sloan."

He eyed her for a moment before he took her hand and held it as if not quite sure how to follow her lead. "Pleased to meet you, Lydia," he finally said.

Their hands remained clasped for several seconds. His eyes never wavered from hers.

Self-conscious, Lydia withdrew from his grasp.

"Seems Katherine was afraid we'd either go naked or starve to death." She pointed to the bags and boxes the teens had delivered. "Bet I can find some coffee in one of these sacks, if you'd like a cup."

"Mind if I take a rain check? I've got a couple more things to do before I call it a day."

Lydia tilted her head. "No rest for the wicked, eh?"

The chief shifted his gaze as Tyler stepped from the hallway and ran to her side.

"Hey there, buddy. How's it going?"

The boy hugged Lydia's leg and shrugged.

Matt smiled, then looked back at Lydia. "There's a community beach not far from here. Safest place to swim on the island."

He pointed toward the large picture windows. Lydia glanced through the glass at the jagged boulders and the ocean beyond.

"Don't know if Ms. O'Connor told you. The water's pretty treacherous in this stretch of the beach. Rocks look peaceful enough, but they're riddled with caves. Easy to get trapped. Tide comes in and they flood out. Rip currents are always a problem."

He glanced at Tyler. "You hear that? Don't play on the boulders. And no swimming unless you're at the community beach."

Lydia watched her son's eyes widen. She didn't want anything else to frighten him. "We don't swim, Mr. Lawson. It won't be a problem."

Matt pursed his lips, then looked back at Lydia. "The Community Church is holding a sand castle contest for the kids at eleven tomorrow. After the morning service. Why don't you meet me at nine for worship. We can go to the contest afterward." He winked at Tyler. "Bet you're strong enough to build a great moat."

Tyler nodded. "I am strong." He drew in a deep breath and stuck out his chest as if trying to prove he was up to the task.

"Bring a bathing suit, and I'll give you a few

swimming lessons after the contest's over," Matt continued.

Was the man hard of hearing? "Mr. Lawson—"

"It's Matt." His dark eyes flashed a no-nonsense look that she was sure could intimidate the most hardened of criminals. Well, it wasn't going to have an effect on her.

Tyler tugged on her arm. "Can we go, Mom?"

"Not to church, honey."

"You could meet me at the park," Matt suggested.

That was the last thing she wanted to do, but she didn't want to disappoint Tyler. A little fun in the sun sounded like what her son needed. What could it hurt?

Plus, she might run into the photographer. She had a few questions that needed to be answered. Had her husband been on the island? And if so, what had brought him to Sanctuary?

Lydia nodded to the chief. "I guess we'll see you about eleven."

Tyler would have a good time, but she'd keep her guard up when it came to Matt Lawson. Law enforcement wasn't to be trusted. That included the security chief.

"Hey, Chief Lawson," the kids called from the picnic area as Matt pulled his pickup into the parking lot the following day.

Six boys, five girls, with probably more petty cash at their disposal than Matt had in his savings. Good kids who could use a little more attention from their jet-set parents. That's why he worked with the church to organize activities. He knew firsthand the change a good role model could make in a kid's life. Not that his family was rich. Far from it. But he'd been on a fast track to nowhere until his church youth director showed Matt the positive impact of putting Christian love into action.

Now, it was payback time.

Plus, he liked kids.

"Savannah and Mark, you team up with Josh. Spread out to the left on the sand." He outlined the spots two more groups would use before he pulled aside the boys he wanted to match up with Tyler.

"You guys ready to build a sand castle?"

They both nodded.

"I'll give you a hand until your teammate arrives. His name's Tyler. He's new on the island, staying at Ms. O'Connor's house." Matt tossed each of the boys a plastic shovel and drew a circle in the sand, outlining the moat. Dropping to his knees next to the boys, he began to dig.

Every few minutes, Matt eyed the road for passing cars.

Where were they? He'd given Lydia directions. Surely she couldn't be lost. The main road ran north and south along the water. No one could miss the beach. Maybe he'd placed too much confidence in her rather hesitant agreement to meet him at the park.

Lydia tried to put up a good front, but under the

surface, she acted like a skittish colt. Something had her spooked big-time. But what?

The kids worked hard, intent on the task at hand. A breeze blew from the water and sea gulls called from overhead. All in all the activity was going well.

So why was he letting a stranger sour his mood? This time, he'd make sure a pretty face didn't lull him off course.

"I thought you wanted me to build the moat," a voice said behind him.

Matt turned to see Tyler standing back from the group, head drooped almost to his chest. Lydia stood next to the child, her arms filled with beach towels.

"Hey, Tyler, I was just helping out until you and your mom arrived. I told the other guys you'd be here soon."

Matt pointed to a boy with red hair and a face full of freckles. "This is Bobby Jackson." He indicated a pudgy boy with a gelled flattop. "And Chase Davenport. Bobby lives next to your great aunt and Chase is two doors down. I thought since you guys are neighbors, it'd be nice for you to work together on the castle."

Bobby handed Tyler a plastic shovel. "You can use this."

"Thanks." Tyler took the shovel and began deepening the moat.

Matt brushed the sand from his hands and knees, nodding to Lydia. "Have any trouble finding us?"

"No problem. We stopped at the library first."

Her hair was pulled into a ponytail, tied with a red ribbon that matched the red shorts and polka-dot blouse she wore. She looked fresh and clean and smelled much sweeter than the kids playing in the sand.

"I wasn't sure we should do this, but—" she glanced at her son "—Tyler really wanted to be here."

"I'm glad you came," Matt said. "Otherwise, I'd be one kid short." He held out his hand for a beach towel. "Need some help?"

"Thanks." She handed him a green towel with pink stripes.

He spread it out not far from where Tyler's team worked, totally absorbed in their project. Lydia sat down.

"May I join you?" he asked.

"Tyler won't mind if you use his towel." She handed him another one, which he spread on the sand.

"You must have left Atlanta in a hurry." Matt tried to sound nonchalant, fishing to catch a tidbit of information.

Lydia shrugged. "A spur-of-the-moment invitation. Katherine thought Tyler and I could use a vacation."

"The woman's got a big heart."

Lydia nodded. "I don't know how I'll ever repay her."

"From what I know of Ms. O'Connor, that's probably the last thing she wants."

Lydia tilted her head and smiled. For an instant, the tension left her face and her eyes twinkled.

Pretty, but with a wary edge. She should be baking cookies and cheering at Little League games, not running from something...or someone.

He shook off the foolish thought and checked his watch. "Ten minutes left to work," he called to the kids before turning back to Lydia. "Some of the parents should be showing up soon. A few of the moms and dads set up grills and cook hot dogs and hamburgers for the kids."

"Is this part of your security chief duties?"

He laughed. "In a roundabout way. Helping kids get a good start in life makes for better citizens in the future."

"So you're helping out?"

"Trying to. The kids are great. And the parents are getting more involved. So far it's been win-win."

Car doors slammed. Matt glanced in the direction of the sound. "There's Chase's dad and Bobby's parents. Nice people. The Jacksons are Katherine's next-door neighbors."

An attractive, thirty-something couple waved to Matt. "Good job, Bobby," the man called out. The boy sprang to his feet and ran to hug his dad.

"It's got a moat and two turrets and it's bigger than the other kids' castles," the boy gushed.

Bobby's mother rumpled her son's red hair and then walked to where Lydia and Matt were rising from the beach towels.

"Sarah Jackson," Matt said. "I'd like you to meet

Lydia Sloan. She and her son, Tyler, are staying at Katherine O'Connor's place for a while."

With a quick smile, warm eyes and auburn hair the color of her son's, Sarah reached out for Lydia's hand. "Welcome to Sanctuary. Bobby's going to love having a friend next door. The two of them can play together."

Matt watched Lydia take a step back. The overt offer of friendship seemed to overwhelm the newcomer.

"We're having a sleepover next Saturday," Sarah continued. "Why don't you let Tyler spend the night?"

"Thanks for inviting him, but I'm…I'm not sure how long we'll be staying here."

"This is my husband, Rob." Sarah turned to greet a solidly built man who walked up to the group.

"Pleased to meet you," he said to Lydia as they shook hands. Turning to Matt, he asked, "Any word on the road repairs?"

"Won't take long once the crew gets started. Right now, they're working on the main county access road. We're next in line. I'll let you know if I hear anything different."

"Sounds good," Rob said.

Luke Davenport stepped forward and extended his hand to Lydia. "I'm Chase's dad. Welcome to Sanctuary."

"Luke's head of the Island Association," Matt added. "He oversees just about everything that happens on Sanctuary."

Luke slapped Matt's back. "Having a good security chief helps."

Matt appreciated the compliment. "Did you get that request I sent over to your office?"

"Don't suppose I could change your mind?"

Matt shook his head. "I told you a year when I signed on."

"Give me a couple weeks." Luke turned to Lydia. "Nice meeting you, ma'am."

Matt glanced at his watch, then walked to the center of the castle-building area and held up his hands.

"Time's up, everyone. Brush yourselves off and then look at what the other teams have done. We'll get the grills going and have some lunch after the announcement of the winning castles."

The smell of charbroiled burgers filled the air a short time later. A number of the parents hovered around the grills, talking about the Friday night storm.

Lydia stood by herself near where Tyler and the boys played.

Matt had asked the church youth director to judge the sand castles and expected him to arrive at any minute. The kids were hungry, but Matt wanted to announce the winner before they gave thanks and got their food.

The youth director pulled into the parking lot. Matt looked up as a black Mercedes zipped along the road, heading south.

"Okay, kids, gather round." The children circled Matt, all except Tyler.

Matt's eyes searched the now-crowded picnic area, but he didn't see Lydia or the boy.

Tires screeched against the blacktop.

Matt glanced around in time to see Lydia's SUV race out of the parking lot, heading north.

FOUR

Lydia pressed her foot down on the accelerator while her hands clutched the steering wheel white-knuckle. She wished she could drive until there were no more men who could steal Tyler away.

And she never wanted to see another black Mercedes again.

Of course, that might be tough on an island full of wealthy home owners. The car could have belonged to an island resident merely out for a drive.

Just like that, she felt foolish for running away. Foolish, tired, scared—the same feelings that had plagued her over these last seven months.

Tyler sat forlornly next to her. His blond hair hung damp with perspiration, the smell of a little boy who'd been hard at play filling the car.

Lydia forced in a deep breath, hoping to quiet her pounding heart and the pulse of blood running rampant through her veins. Would she react this way every time she saw a black Mercedes?

Checking her speed, Lydia eased her foot from the gas pedal. "Tyler?"

The boy stared straight ahead.

"I'm sorry we had to leave."

Tyler's fingers twisted around the buckle of his seatbelt. "Was he wearing an Action-Pac watch?"

"Who, honey?"

"The man in the black car."

A chill ran down Lydia's spine. "Did the man in the school yard wear one?"

Tyler nodded, his eyes wide, his forehead wrinkled with worry. "An A.P. digital. I didn't see his face, but I saw his watch when he tried to grab me."

Lydia's stomach roiled at the memory of that frightful afternoon. Before this, Tyler had never mentioned a watch. Another clue, but would it help her find the man who tried to grab her son?

"You know, honey, sometimes I overreact. Now that I think about it, that wasn't the same car as in Atlanta. And the driver wasn't wearing a watch."

No way she could have seen the man's wrist, but she needed to reassure her son.

Tyler's lower lip inched forward in a pout. "Then why'd we have to leave?"

Lydia sighed. How could she explain her immediate panic? Seeing the car had made her heart pound with fear. Her only thought had been to protect Tyler. So she'd pulled him from the beach activity.

Now, the look on her son's face made Lydia realize her mistake. From here on, she needed to remain calm. Sanctuary Island was far from Atlanta. She and Tyler were safe here. At least for a while.

"I know you wanted to stay longer."

He scrubbed a sandy hand across his face and captured the tear trailing down his cheek. "Bobby and Chase said we did the best. We could've won."

Tyler needed stability and security, not a mother who ran scared. She smiled reassuringly. "I'm glad you had a good time."

"Can I see Bobby again?"

"Maybe later." A normal life, that's what Tyler deserved, filled with friends and fun.

"Bobby said he's having some of the guys over next Saturday. He invited me."

Lydia's throat constricted. She swallowed the lump threatening to shut off her airway. She wasn't ready to let Tyler out of her sight for an hour, let alone a whole night. "We'll see," was all she could promise.

Turning into Katherine's driveway, Lydia felt an unexpected sense of coming home. The house that loomed ominously two nights ago seemed like a safe refuge in the light of day.

Birds flittered in the trees, chirping a welcome song as a rambunctious squirrel dug for nuts at the foot of the live oak tree. At the far edge of the lawn, brick-red begonias nestled next to azalea bushes, thick with blooms, while purple periwinkles fluttered in the breeze.

"Get the library books from the backseat," Lydia told Tyler as she pulled the key from the ignition.

"Bobby doesn't have schoolwork. He's on vacation."

Lydia smiled. "But you're not. Your school is still in session. At least for another two weeks. You're on…" She thought for a minute. "A sabbatical."

Tyler scrunched up his face. "What's that?"

"It's time away from your regular work so you can concentrate on special projects."

"Was that what you were doing on the computer at the library?"

Lydia sighed. She hated lying, but she never wanted her child to know about his father's nefarious activities.

"I've got an idea for a project I think you should do."

Tyler's shoulders slumped as he grabbed the books from the backseat, slammed the door and sighed. "More work."

"Would a PB&J make it better?"

His face brightened. "Yum!"

Lydia had just handed Tyler his sandwich when the phone rang. She tensed. Who would be calling?

Slowly, she raised the phone to her ear and smiled with relief when she heard Katherine's hello.

"How's your sister-in-law?" Lydia asked immediately.

"Feisty and stubborn. The doctor said her progress is remarkable."

"Because you're there to help. You've been so thoughtful to us, as well, Katherine. Clothing and toys for Tyler, groceries—"

"Enough of that. I knew you'd never use my credit

card. I decided to take the situation into my own hands. Besides, we're family. And that's what families do. Help one another."

"How can I ever thank you?"

"By taking care of yourself and Tyler. You've been through so much. Use this time to heal."

Tears stung Lydia's eyes. She blinked to keep them from spilling down her cheeks, grateful Tyler had gone into the living room to play.

"I know what you had to put up with when it came to Sonny," Katherine said.

"He tried to be a good father. It was the husband role that seemed to be the problem."

"I blame his upbringing. And that sister of mine who ran off and left him as a child. Then his father thought he could raise him and wouldn't ask for my help. Without God in his life, Sonny never learned about sacrifice and commitment. Tell me, dear, were you ever happy?"

The question caught Lydia off guard.

"At first everything seemed good. Maybe I was naive. We were young and poor."

Despite their differences, she and Sonny had made the best of a bad situation. Until the day she had walked into his office and discovered the vile pictures on his computer screen.

Change of subject. "You know, Katherine, I saw some photos on a bulletin board in the Community Center."

"Joel Cowan's work. He's the island photo bug."

"Funny, but a man in one of the pictures looked like Sonny."

"Why that's odd. Sonny always said he was too busy to visit the island."

"But he encouraged you to move here."

"That's right, dear. After Patrick died. Sonny said a man he worked with knew about the gated community. Although Sonny never implied he'd been to Sanctuary."

If Sonny hadn't visited Katherine, then what had he been doing on the island? And who was the other man in the photo?

"My mistake, no doubt," Lydia said. "I hope you can relax a bit while you're in Ireland. See some of the sights."

"Actually, one of the neighbors took me for a nice ride today. A gentleman about my age. He's been so thoughtful. I invited him to join us for dinner. I must say I'm enjoying his company."

Lydia smiled, happy for the woman who seemed more like *her* aunt than Sonny's.

"Wouldn't hurt you to look around, Lydia. Find someone to make your days a little brighter. In due time, of course."

Matt Lawson's smiling face as he worked with the children on the beach came to mind. Lydia shook off the thought and concentrated on what Katherine was saying.

"Tell that sweet grandnephew of mine to go next door and meet Bobby Jackson. They're about the same age. Sarah and Rob are good folks."

"The boys are already friends." Lydia told Katherine about the contest and the fun on the beach.

"I'm glad he had a good time. By the way, the Community Church is on the mainland, just off the Bay Road. Nice congregation. When you're ready."

"Matt mentioned it."

Katherine gave Lydia her phone number in Ireland. "Your cell won't work transatlantic."

"Stupid of me, but I forgot it in Atlanta," Lydia admitted. Really stupid. In her rush to pick up Tyler, she'd left the phone at the police station.

"No problem, just call direct. And hug Tyler for me."

Lydia hung up, wondering about the Community Church Katherine mentioned. Matt said he helped with the youth program. Not what she expected from a former cop. But then, she had a jaded view of law enforcement.

"Can I play on the beach, Mom?" Tyler called from the living room.

"*May* I," Lydia corrected. "Let's take a walk instead. The fresh air will do us both good. I'll get a plastic bag. We can collect shells."

Lydia turned on the security alarm and locked the door behind them. Tyler grabbed his Frisbee off the picnic table and stopped at the edge of the deck where he sloughed off his shoes, then skipped ahead to the beach, spraying a fine stream of white sand with each footfall.

He kicked his feet in the waves and splashed cool

saltwater on Lydia's legs as she neared. Giggling with glee, he tossed his Frisbee into the air and raced to catch the flying disc before it landed.

"Not too far into the water," Lydia warned as he ran through the surf.

Bobby's house sat next to Katherine's. The brick two-story had a wide deck that led down to a terraced yard where a children's climber filled the grassy knoll.

Two houses south, they passed what Matt had said was Chase's home, a grand Tudor that sat back from the beach. Three more palatial dwellings peered at them through the foliage of live oaks and tall pines as they continued along the shore.

Pointing to a bed of colorful shells, Lydia pulled the plastic bag from her pocket. "Let's collect seashells."

The bag was half-full when someone called to them.

Looking up, she shaded her eyes and saw a pink stucco three-story home rimmed in decks with wrought iron railings. A pool, gazebo and formal garden decorated the backyard where a tall, slender man stood on a lookout platform that separated the beach from the lush lawn.

"I heard I had new neighbors. You must be Lydia Sloan," he called down from his perch.

News traveled fast on the island, she thought as he descended the stairs and jogged toward them.

Wide smile. Warm eyes.

"Joel Cowan." He stretched out his hand.

The photographer? Had fate brought her face-to-face with the man who might know something about her husband? Or had her prayers for help finally been answered? Hard to believe the Almighty would be giving her a break.

No matter who or what deserved the credit, Lydia returned the handshake.

"I stopped by the Davenports just as Luke and his boy came home from the beach," the photographer said.

Tyler stepped forward. "Did Chase say we won the sand castle contest?"

Joel nodded. "Matter of fact, he did."

"Really?" Her son's eyes bugged open. "We won? Did you hear that, Mom?"

"Chase said Bobby has your prize."

Tyler yanked on Lydia's arm. "Come on, Mom. Let's go get it!"

Before she had a chance to answer, Tyler started backtracking along the beach.

"Tyler, wait—"

He stopped. "Mom, hurry!"

She held up her finger. "In a minute."

Lydia turned back to Joel. "I saw your photographs on the bulletin board at the Community Center."

Joel beamed with pride. "Hobby of mine, but people seem to enjoy my work. I'd love to take a few shots of you and your son. Water in the background." He glanced down at the wedding ring on Lydia's left hand. "Nice gift for your husband."

"I'm widowed, Mr. Cowan."

"Sorry to hear that. And it's Joel."

She nodded. "In my opinion, Joel, you've got talent. Those photos captured island life—the water, wildlife. I especially liked the shot of the seagulls."

"Down by the marina?"

"I'm not sure where it was taken. The man in the background looked familiar. Hard to tell with only a small snapshot."

"I've got the negative. Be glad to print an enlargement for you."

"That's very kind. Thank you, Joel."

"Come on, Mom," Tyler called.

"Mind if I walk with you?" Joel asked.

"Well, I—"

He smiled, good-naturedly. "A little exercise will do me good."

As much as Lydia didn't want company, civility might be the best tactic. She didn't want to insult one of Katherine's neighbors and she needed to find out more about the photo. Joel seemed like a gregarious type of guy. Hopefully, she'd learn more about Sonny's secret trip to Sanctuary.

Tyler dashed ahead, tossing his Frisbee as he ran, while she and Joel followed at a more leisurely pace.

"I've enjoyed getting to know your aunt," Joel said. "Katherine moved here a few months after I did. Isn't she visiting a relative in Ireland?"

"Her sister-in-law had a hip replacement. Katherine wanted to help out."

Joel's face broke into a smirk. "When she gets

back, I'll give her a hard time for never mentioning her attractive niece."

Lydia pretended she didn't hear his comment.

He pulled in a deep breath. "Quite a storm we had Friday night."

An understatement to say the least. Lydia had driven through high winds, torrential rain and lightning that lit up the sky.

"The men at the picnic said the Bay Road almost flooded. Any danger we'd be stranded on the island?" she asked.

Joel shrugged. "You never know. Most folks keep a boat at the marina on the north end of Sanctuary just in case. If the road floods, they boat over to the mainland. Rob Jackson's got a beauty—thirty-six-foot Stingray."

"Bobby's dad?"

Joel nodded, then pointed to the Jackson home directly ahead. "There's Bobby now."

The boy was playing on the climber. When he saw Tyler, he waved and raced down to the beach.

"Guess what?" Bobby yelled. "We won! First place for our age group." He pulled fluorescent green goggles from his pocket and handed them to Tyler. "We each got a prize. I got yours."

"Thanks!" Tyler turned to Lydia. "Can Bobby come over to our house?"

"Of course." Lydia looked at the redhead. "Why don't you tell your mom and dad where you're going, Bobby?"

"Here, use my phone." Joel handed his cell to the boy, who quickly punched in the numbers and talked to his mother before returning it to Joel.

"Mom said I can play for an hour, Mrs. Sloan."

Tyler nudged his new friend. "Race you to the door." The boys took off.

Joel glanced toward the house. "Katherine told me she had her deck refinished. I've been thinking about doing the same to mine. Mind if I take a look?"

After Katherine's generosity, how could Lydia refuse a neighbor's request? "Of course, Joel."

As they neared the house, Lydia pulled the key from her pocket.

"Can I do the alarm?" Tyler asked.

She turned the key and shoved the door open. "Remember the code?"

"Sure."

"Mr. Cowan and I will be on the deck. Why don't you show Bobby the toys Katherine sent you?"

The buzz of the security alarm being disabled drifted into the backyard.

Joel spent the next few minutes inspecting the deck.

"Looks like the contractor did a good job. I'll give him a call." Joel sat on one of the Adirondack lawn chairs across from Lydia.

"What line of business are you in?" she asked, breathing in the warm salt air and enjoying the view of the water.

"Actually, Lydia, I'm a lawyer by trade. I owned a rather large firm in Jacksonville until I got tired of the daily grind." He crossed his legs and chuckled. "Checked my bank balance and decided I didn't have to work."

Wealth had its privileges, and Joel seemed eager to talk about his good fortune. Keeping an ego in check must be difficult surrounded by the lavish trappings of island life.

Although, Katherine never spoke of money or the status it sometimes bought.

Lydia thought of Matt Lawson playing with the children. He didn't seem the type to be swayed by money or power, either.

"Don't listen to the women on the island." Joel winked. "They're taking bets as to when I'll get married. Everyone's a matchmaker these days."

Lydia forced a smile, but her thoughts remained on the security chief. She hadn't noticed a wedding ring on *his* left hand. Not that she had been looking, of course.

"Doubt a woman would put up with me," Joel rambled. "I spend my days sailing. Entertain friends most weekends with gourmet meals or parties that are the talk of the island. Travel whenever wanderlust hits."

Joel checked his watch and rubbed his hands together.

"Listen, I've overstayed my welcome. Promise me you'll stop by whenever you're on my end of the beach. In fact, I'm having a few friends over for a party next Saturday. I'd be honored if you'd join us.

I could enlarge that picture you're interested in seeing and have it for you that night."

Dating and parties were the last thing on her mind. She'd arrange to pick up the photo some other time. "Thanks, but—"

Footsteps sounded behind her.

Joel glanced up. His eyes bugged open. "What the—"

Lydia turned and gasped.

Matt Lawson rounded the corner of the house.

"What are you doing here?" Lydia pushed out of her chair, the hair on the back of her neck rising in protest.

Matt held a gun in his hand, and it appeared to be aimed at her.

FIVE

Lowering his weapon, Matt glared first at the lawyer and then at Lydia.

"Put that gun away this instant," she demanded, her eyes stern, her face drained of color. "Children are in the house."

Joel jumped to his feet and held up his hands, palms out. "Look, old boy, no need to go ballistic."

Matt holstered his weapon and stepped onto the deck. He wasn't interested in anything Joel had to say.

"Sorry to scare you, Lydia. Your alarm went off. It's silent on your end. A protective feature, in case there's trouble." Matt glanced at Joel. "*Is* there trouble?"

Joel took a step forward. "I've had enough of this, Lawson. Ever since I moved to Sanctuary, you've been giving me a hard time."

"I do a basic background check on all residents before we install a security system. No reason to be upset, sir, unless you've got something to hide."

The lawyer pointed a finger at Matt. "That does it. I'm calling Luke Davenport."

"Please," Lydia said. "Sit down so I can talk to the chief."

Joel stepped back to the deck chair but remained standing.

"Tyler must have tripped the alarm," Lydia said to Matt. "We took a walk on the beach and met Joel. When we got back to the house, Tyler and Bobby wanted to play inside. I'm sure Tyler wasn't aware he hit the wrong buttons."

"Mind if I talk to him?" Matt asked.

"You don't believe me?"

He raked his free hand through his hair and sighed. The woman got under his skin.

"I'd like to explain the alarm system. To both of you. So you'll know how it works in case you ever have a problem."

She opened the sliding-glass door and called Tyler. The boys appeared almost immediately.

"Bobby and I are hungry, Mom."

"Say hello to Chief Lawson."

"Hey, Chief." Tyler stepped onto the deck, then dug his hand in his pocket and pulled out the goggles. "Bobby gave me my prize. Thanks."

Matt smiled. The kid got to him, too, but in a good way. "Tyler, your mom said you disarmed the security alarm today."

The boy's eyes widened. "Yes, sir."

"You touched a couple of buttons that activate a special alarm. I'll explain it to you and your mom."

Matt didn't want to frighten the child, but it was important he understood the feature.

"Like if there's a bad guy walking around outside?" Tyler asked.

Matt glanced momentarily at Joel. "Bad guy? That's right, Tyler. If you want me to come protect you, but don't want the bad person to know, you can tap in the special code."

"Cool."

"It's not something to play with. You understand that, don't you?"

Bobby stuck his head out the door. "It was an accident, Chief Lawson. Tyler's hand slipped. We've got the same system at my house."

Bobby turned to Lydia. "Mrs. Sloan, I forgot my mom said to remind you Tyler's invited to my sleepover next Saturday night. Can Tyler come? Please?"

"I'll call her tomorrow. Why don't you two get some cookies and milk?"

The boys hustled into the kitchen. Cabinets banged and plates clattered as they helped themselves to the snack.

"Let's talk in the house," Matt told Lydia, then peered at Joel. "Privately."

Lydia hesitated for half a second before turning to her guest. "If you'll excuse me for a minute."

The lawyer bowed his head. "Of course, my dear."

Cowan knew how to turn on the charm. Surely Ms. O'Connor wouldn't want Lydia involved with the conniving playboy. In deference to the older woman, Matt felt obliged to set Lydia straight.

"Bobby, finish your cookies and milk while Chief Lawson talks to Tyler and me for a few minutes." Lydia led the way through the kitchen.

Bobby nodded before he shoved another cookie into his open mouth.

Wiping the back of his hand over his lips, Tyler hopped from his chair and followed Lydia and Matt toward the alarm keypad at the entrance to the house.

She leaned against the wall while Matt explained the system. He spoke slowly, detailing the features so her son could understand.

Although appreciative of his patience with Tyler, she was troubled by another thought. Why did the security chief keep appearing at the most unexpected times? Was he merely doing his job? Or was there another reason?

Until she knew for sure, she'd watch her step.

"Push these two buttons and the signal will sound in my office," he explained to Tyler.

"And what if you're in your truck?" Lydia interrupted.

"Don't worry." Matt looked deep into her eyes. "I'll get the message."

Tyler pretended to tap in the special code. Satisfied he understood the system, he raced back to the kitchen for more cookies.

Matt stepped toward Lydia.

She tilted her head and looked up at him. The fresh lime scent of his aftershave tickled her nose. Too close for comfort, she crossed her arms over her chest and moved back. After all, the guy had come calling with a gun.

"I always seem a step off," he said, looking ill at ease. "But I like that little guy of yours. Reminds me of a boy back in Miami."

Lydia remembered seeing the picture on the wall in his office. Was that who he was talking about?

"And I like Ms. O'Connor," Matt continued. "She's a good Christian woman."

Lydia stared back at him. Where was he headed? By the looks of his body language, he appeared almost apologetic.

"But I've got to tell you. That man on your deck is bad news."

Lydia narrowed her eyes. "What?"

"You don't want him hanging around."

She dropped her hands and squared her shoulders.

"Mr. Cowan seems like a very nice man." Lydia feigned a cordial tone of voice. Inside, she was fuming. The chief was taking this whole security role way too far. First, he acted like Robo Cop with the drawn gun, and now he was giving advice like Dr. Phil.

"Seems money's a little too easy to come by for a guy who's unemployed," Matt said.

"He was a lawyer in Jacksonville. He sold his business to have more free time."

"He told you that? A lawyer in Jacksonville?"

"Joel stopped working to have more time to entertain his friends." The explanation seemed lame even to her ears.

"Now that's a good one." Matt laughed. Then he wiped the smirk from his face and pointed a finger at her. "You want my advice? Don't get involved with him."

She stuck out her jaw and glared at Matt. "But then, I didn't *ask* for your advice, did I, Chief Lawson?"

She stared at him for half a minute, hoping he got the message that telling her what to do was the wrong tactic. Then turning about-face, she strode toward the sliding-glass door.

Joel stood when she stepped onto the deck.

"You mentioned something about next Saturday?" Lydia made her voice sweet as iced tea doused with sugar. She wasn't interested in going to a party, but at least, she'd be able to view the enlarged photo. Plus, Matt needed to be taught a lesson.

Joel nodded. "I hope you'll join me."

Matt came up beside her. She slanted a look at his face, pleased to see it pulled tight with frustration.

Smiling coyly, she added a bit of a Southern drawl to her reply. "Why, Joel, how nice. I'd love to spend the evening with you."

Matt's neck turned red as he growled with displeasure. "Looks like I'm finished here," he said before turning on his heels and leaving the deck the way he had entered.

As he stomped away, an immediate sense of loss

overwhelmed Lydia. She'd made a point of letting Matt know he'd overstepped his bounds. So why did she feel so mixed-up inside?

On the drive back to his office, the cool air from the open window helped clear Matt's mind and soothe his temper.

Lydia didn't seem like a party girl who allowed money to twist her heart. If she wanted to carouse around with Joel Cowan, Matt sure couldn't stop her.

Just so Tyler wouldn't be caught in the middle.

Like Enrico.

Give me a second chance, Lord.

Once at his desk, Matt couldn't work. He stared at the photo on the wall. Enrico was fatherless because Matt had made a bad decision. Guilt still ate at him.

He checked his desk calendar. His partner's son had turned eight the beginning of last month. Matt had been too busy to call. Or so he told himself. Truth was, he didn't want to open old wounds.

Pain he could take. Self-condemnation was harder to handle.

Sucking in a deep breath, he reached for the phone and dialed Miami. Connie Rodriquez answered on the second ring.

"It's Matt."

"Long time since we've heard your voice," she said. "Enrico misses you."

Regret tore at Matt's heart. "How's he doing?"

"Better. You know kids, they adapt."

"Wish him a belated happy birthday for me."

"He got the catcher's mitt you sent."

Matt smiled. "How's his team?"

"Four-and-0."

"Pete would have been proud," Matt said.

"That's what I keep telling Enrico."

Matt hesitated for a moment before asking, "What about you, Connie?"

"Me?"

He could envision her shrugging her slender shoulders, remembering the way her life had been when she had a husband.

"Life goes on. God called one of us home. He left me behind to take care of our son. It's enough for now."

Matt's throat thickened. He tried to swallow the lump that formed. "I'm…I'm sorry."

"I told you before, Matt, I don't blame you. You didn't kill my Pedro."

"Yeah, but—"

"No, buts. It happened, for whatever reason. We have to go on. That means you, too, before the guilt eats a hole in your heart."

"Redemption doesn't come easy."

"I'll pray for you, Matt, that you can earn your redemption."

Matt hung up, burdened with all that had happened. A long jog would clear his head, chase away the memories. At least for a while.

Picking up the phone again, he called the dispatcher. "Eunice, put me through to Jason."

"Yeah, boss?" the kid answered.

"I'll be out of the office for about an hour. Head over to the marina and make sure the area's secure. I'll have Eunice patch any calls to your cell."

"Roger. Out."

Matt changed into shorts and a T-shirt, laced up his running shoes and headed for the beach.

He ran along the water's edge. Warmed by the sun and the exertion, he allowed his mind to dwell on nothing except the surf pounding against the shore. The water worked magic with him.

He passed Cowan's property. Matt would like to be a fly on that guy's wall. Joel had moved to Sanctuary a year ago. Shortly after Matt got wind of a drug operation setting up shop on one of the Georgia islands.

A little background check on the playboy newcomer paid off. Three years ago, Joel had been arrested for possession of a controlled substance. Pain medication for an old back injury, or so Joel claimed. The offense earned him thirty days in jail, two-hundred-fifty hours of community service and two years probation.

Too much of a coincidence in Matt's mind, especially when Joel paid cash for one of the most expensive homes on the island, then bought a top-of-the-line sailboat, the envy of every mariner for miles around. He filled his three-car garage with two Beemers and a Jag, threw elaborate parties and liked his women tall, blond and well-endowed.

Although all the residents enjoyed a privileged

lifestyle, Joel Cowan seemed extravagant even by Sanctuary standards. And Matt couldn't find a source for all that wealth. Made him wonder if the guy wasn't involved in something illegal. But Matt needed proof.

He glanced back at Joel's house just as a woman stepped onto the deck. Another trophy for the island's Casanova.

Please God, don't let Lydia get involved with him.

Funny to find her chatting with Joel today when she seemed so reserved at the beach. Matt needed to do a little checking on his own. See what he could dig up on the pretty widow's husband, as well.

Returning to the office, Matt showered and changed into a fresh uniform. He had converted a back room into his living quarters, preferring to sleep there rather than in an apartment miles away on the mainland.

A few people called him a workaholic. He wouldn't deny the accusation. But he had a job to do and people to protect.

His first phone call was to tell Jason he was back at his desk. Matt had taken a chance hiring the kid three months ago. So far it had paid off. Jason had a fierce determination to do what was right and an unfailing loyalty to Matt for giving him his first job in law enforcement. If the kid had a flaw, it was an exuberant enthusiasm that sometimes got in the way of sound judgment.

The second call was to the Marina Coffee Shop. Matt ordered a pastrami on rye, fries and a milk shake to be delivered, fully prepared to spend two or three hours catching up on paperwork.

Halfway through the sandwich, the phone rang.

"Security, Lawson."

"Chief?"

Recognizing the woman's voice, Matt struggled to keep from emitting a groan. "What can I do for you, Muriel?"

Sanctuary Island's head librarian reminded him of an old busybody schoolmarm.

"Somebody stick a romance novel in with the encyclopedias?" He couldn't resist teasing her.

She cleared her throat. "For your information, I set up that children's book club you wanted for the summer."

"Glad to hear it, Muriel. The kids will love it."

"Kids I can handle. It's the teenage boys that give me fits. What about those two who were looking at the girlie pictures on the computer last week? You happen to talk to their father?"

"The dad promised he'd handle it. Doubt you'll be seeing either of them online for a while."

"If only." She sighed. "You know how I feel about the Internet."

"Good grief, Muriel, it's the twenty-first century. Computers are a part of our lives."

"Easy for you to say," she huffed. "If you'd seen what I did today, you'd change your opinion, quick 'nough."

"More boys ogling girls?"

"As a matter of fact, someone did access a pornography site."

Matt reached for the rest of his sandwich. "Give me the boy's name."

"It wasn't one of the teenagers, this time, Chief. It was an adult. 'Course there's no law against what she was viewing. But I just don't like it."

Matt dropped his sandwich back on the foam take-out box. "She?"

"Yes, sir. New to the island. Her name's Lydia Sloan."

SIX

Matt hung up the phone and tossed the rest of his sandwich in the trash. He'd lost his appetite.

Why would Lydia Sloan log on to a pornography Web site? Although he hadn't known her long, she seemed like a decent person. If she'd accessed a porn site, there had to be a reason. But what?

For the life of him, Matt didn't have a clue.

He rubbed his forehead and thought of Tyler. The boy deserved a mom who baked cookies and helped with school projects.

Life could be so complicated, especially for a kid who just wanted to be loved.

Matt knew that all too well.

Not that he hadn't survived.

Cut Lydia a wide berth, his voice of reason whispered.

Easier said than done.

He shook his head and grabbed a folder from his in-box. Sam Snyder's request for retirement. The gate guard wanted to spend the rest of his days cruising the island in his new motorboat, catching whatever happened to nibble at his line.

Matt couldn't blame him. Sam was a good man with a big heart, but his performance had slipped over the last few months. Like the night of the storm. Sam had left the gate open and the guardhouse unmanned while he checked the embankment. The water was rising, but he never called for help.

If Matt hadn't sent Jason to look for the old guy, no telling how long the entrance would have gone unmanned.

Matt had given Sam the benefit of the doubt on more than one occasion. If the situation continued, he'd be forced to let the older assistant go. Retirement seemed a better solution.

Matt signed the form and forwarded it to the Island Association for their approval.

Losing Sam meant one less set of eyes and hands to share the workload. Matt wouldn't leave the island shorthanded. But he didn't want to twiddle his thumbs in Sanctuary any longer than necessary. He promised Connie he'd find Pete's killer. He wouldn't let her down again.

Reaching for the phone, Matt tapped in the number to the Atlanta Police Department and asked to speak to Detective Roger Harris.

"Son of a gun," Harris said when he got on the line. "Never thought I'd hear your voice again. Where are you?"

Matt stretched back in his chair and ran his free

hand through his hair. "Would you believe Georgia? On the coast. I'm chief of security for Sanctuary Island."

Harris let out a whistle. "I'm impressed. Hobnobbing with the wealthy. Not bad, not bad at all."

"I wouldn't call it hobnobbing. More like responding when their security alarms go off." A vision of Lydia standing in Ms. O'Connor's kitchen floated through his mind.

"Definitely a step up from investigating drug lords on the streets of Miami."

Matt shifted in his chair.

"You always loved the work," Harris continued. "Not like most of us looking for an easy way out. You hear Smith and Paris left the same time I did?"

"They ever find evidence on Paris?"

"Negative. He's working here in Atlanta."

"Not my favorite guy."

"Ditto," Harris added. "'Course none of us compared with you, Matt. You were the best. And you know how I felt about Rodriquez."

"Yeah, well…" A tightness filled Matt's chest. Fourteen months and he still couldn't get around it.

Clearing his throat, he forced his mind back to the issue at hand. "Listen, I'll be short a man before long and wondered if you knew anyone who might like to move to the coast. Maybe a guy on pension with a few good years left. The pay's not bad and it's usually nice and quiet down here."

"Matter of fact, someone does come to mind. Butch Griffin. Twenty-year man. Retired about a year ago. Took a security job for a large computer firm. The company downsized, and Butch's looking for work. I'll give him a call, if you'd like. The guy's good. Keeps his nose clean. And knows his stuff. How soon do you need him?"

"I'll notify the Island Association. Should be able to put him to work as soon as he gets here."

Matt appreciated the recommendation. Maybe he could stay on track with his departure plans if a new hire shared the load. Meanwhile, it wouldn't hurt to bait Harris and see what he caught.

"The name Sloan mean anything to you?"

Harris hesitated. "Yeah, why?"

"We had a stranger pass through these parts not too long ago. Weird guy. Fulton County plates, only he says he hasn't been to Atlanta in months. No APB out on him so I didn't call you."

Matt stretched the truth. If the Sloan name was tied to anything suspect, Harris would know.

The detective expelled a deep breath, then laughed. "Wouldn't be the same Sloan we're interested in unless your stranger was about five-six, blond and answered to the name of Lydia. The story was all over the Atlanta papers. Arson case."

Matt sat up straight. "Yeah?"

"Husband died in the blaze. Wife and kid made it to safety. About seven months ago. Nothing to go on, but there's speculation the wife torched the place."

"Insurance?"

"Enough. Seems she upped the limits on the house

just the week before. With his life insurance, she'd be sitting pretty, except for the question of arson. Now, she's skipped town. No one seems to know where she went. Or why she disappeared."

Matt felt the back of his neck tingle. Had Lydia started the fire that killed her husband? If not, then why did she leave Atlanta and head for the seclusion of Sanctuary? Was she running scared? Or on the run for another reason?

"What'd the arson investigation come up with?" Matt asked.

"Nothing concrete."

"So you haven't put out an APB on her?"

"Not yet," the cop replied.

Matt knew he should tip Harris off to Lydia's whereabouts, but he kept his mouth shut. He'd do a little investigating on his own.

Matt shook his head as he hung up the phone.

From what he'd seen, Lydia's son came first in her life. If she had set the fire, surely she would have ensured Tyler was far from home. No, she wasn't an arsonist.

But she *was* hiding from something or someone.

"I love you, honey," Lydia whispered to Tyler as she tucked him into bed that night. She left the door open so the light from the hallway shone into his room. Ever since the fire, he was afraid to sleep in the dark. Not that she blamed him.

Lydia had a hard time sleeping, as well. She

usually awoke with the memory of smoke filling her nostrils. Some nights, the fire seemed so real her eyes burned and she shook with fright.

She told herself it was only a dream. But the nervous quiver in her stomach wouldn't stop until she made her rounds. She'd peek in on Tyler, then check each room to ensure a fire wasn't flaming out of control.

Had she turned off the oven? Could a candle be burning? Perhaps the charcoal grill had overturned and hot briquettes were sparking into something dangerous.

Every night her search found nothing amiss. No fire, no smoke, no reason to be alarmed. Relieved, she'd end up in Tyler's room, looking down at her precious little boy.

Why had they been saved seven months ago? Somehow she'd awakened with her only thought of getting Tyler to safety. She still didn't know how she'd managed to carry him through the flames.

She'd like to think God had interceded on their behalf. But after all that happened, how could she believe He had listened to her cries for help? More important people had His ear, not a woman who had made a mess of her marriage—and her life.

Tears formed in Lydia's eyes and spilled down her cheeks. She walked into the kitchen, grabbed a tissue and wiped it over her face. Would she ever be free of the terrifying memory of that night?

Someone had entered their house and started the blaze. But who?

Ruby hoped to find something when she went through the records at the club. A long shot. And Lydia wouldn't hold her breath it would pay off. She needed to keep digging. Once she knew who was responsible for Sonny's death, she'd know who was after her son.

Ruby had mentioned the investigative reporter. Trish Delaney might provide some answers.

Lydia dug through her purse for the phone number and dialed.

"*Atlanta Journal-Constitution.* Delaney." The woman answered with a raspy smoker's voice piled on top of a country twang.

"This is…" Lydia hesitated. "This is Lydia Sloan. You said I could call anytime day or night."

"I remember. The Men's Club."

"When you phoned before, I thought I could find what I needed on my own. Things have changed, and I'd like your help."

"I've done a little checking, Mrs. Sloan. Word was, your husband wanted out. Is that right?"

Lydia sighed. "At first I didn't know what he was involved in. He told me it was freelance work. He was a computer technician. Worked on Web sites. I never thought it was anything like this."

"How'd you find out?"

"He had an office at home. I walked in and saw one of the pictures on his monitor." Lydia paused. "Made me sick."

"Of course it did."

"I wanted to leave him that night, but we have a son. Sonny promised to end it."

"So you stayed?" the reporter prompted.

"I gave him ten days. He said he'd find a way out. First, he had to gather evidence. Said they'd kill him if he walked away without having something he could hold over their heads."

"Who are *they*, Mrs. Sloan?"

"I...I don't know."

"And what happened?"

"He died nine days later."

"Any idea what he found?"

"Not a clue. He must have known they were on to him. He even had me up the insurance on our house. After his death, I went through his papers and computer files. Nothing. One night, he was mugged leaving the club. Two days later, someone tried to run him off the road."

"Did he recognize the car?"

"A black Mercedes. I did some checking. The car had to have been scratched or dented so I called dealers for their service records. Then, I contacted all the garages in the surrounding area, but nothing turned up. I even hired a private detective who ran scared once he got wind people in high places were involved in the club."

"Pretty much a dead end."

"I've tried every angle I could think of and haven't gotten anywhere. Can you help me?"

"Any idea where your husband might have hid the incriminating evidence?"

"Under their noses."

"What do you mean?"

"A year ago, Sonny lost a good job when he played a little trick on his CEO. He buried a very inflammatory joke on the company Web site. Guess the other I.T. guys got a kick out of it until someone leaked the information."

"So the boss was ticked?"

"He fired Sonny."

"What are you saying, Mrs. Sloan?"

"Since my husband used his computer skills before to hide a joke on the Web, he may have tried the same technique again."

"You think he planted evidence of the corruption on the Men's Club Web site?" Trish Delaney sounded incredulous.

"I know it seems odd. And so far, I haven't found anything. Call it woman's intuition, but I keep getting the feeling that's where I need to look."

"Interesting. And unique. I'll access the site. See what I can find. Give me a little time."

"I'll call you," Lydia said.

She hung up feeling more optimistic than she had in months. Trish Delaney had the contacts and expertise to accomplish what Lydia couldn't. As much as she didn't want her story turned into front-page news, someone had tried to hurt Tyler. That upped the stakes.

Lydia filled the teapot with water and pulled a

teabag from the cabinet. She needed to distance herself from all that had happened in Atlanta. A good book and a cup of herbal raspberry would soothe her troubled spirit.

The pot whistled. Lydia poured the boiling water and, cup in hand, walked back to a small, tiled sitting area off the master bedroom.

A noise caused her to look up at the narrow window over the writing desk.

She screamed.

The cup dropped from her hands and shattered on the cold tile floor.

SEVEN

After his conversation with Harris, Matt logged on to the *AJC*s Web site and double clicked on Archives. Tapping in a time line and the key words Sonny Sloan, he hit Search. Three articles flashed on the screen. Matt saved them to a disc and printed a hard copy.

Harris had been right. According to the stories, Sonny died in a house fire seven months ago. Lydia and her son had escaped. Two residents of the middle-class Atlanta neighborhood said Lydia had packed her car with personal belongings and parked it in the driveway the night of the fire.

Matt ran a hand over his forehead. If she didn't know about the fire, why'd she pack her car? It didn't make sense.

Unless she was planning to leave the next morning.

He shoved the papers into his top desk drawer, scooted his chair back and started to stand when the phone rang.

"Security. Lawson."

"Chief, it's Luke Davenport. My wife just got

home from the gals' neighborhood bridge party. Said she heard noise down on the beach. Probably teens. Remember that problem we had last summer?"

"Bonfires and booze. Yeah, I remember. Mrs. Davenport see anyone?"

"Just heard noise, that's all. Maybe we're over-reacting, but after that problem they're having on the mainland—"

"I'll check it out. Call me if you hear or see anything else."

"Thanks, Chief. Appreciate your help."

Matt hung up, then rang Eunice.

"Where's Jason?"

"In the marina area," the dispatcher said.

"Have him drive south along the beach. Tell him to be on the lookout for teens having a little late-night fun. I'll drive north and meet him en route."

Matt climbed into his pickup and headed for the beach access road. Lowering his headlights, he rolled down the window and listened. Water lapped against the shore.

Low tide.

Quiet. Peaceful.

He stopped at the Davenport property line and turned on his searchlight. No movement. Nothing out of place in the serene seaside setting.

Easing his foot down on the accelerator, he drove past Joel Cowan's home, dark against the night sky.

Strange.

Most of the residents spotlighted their homes at

night. Maybe Cowan liked entertaining his lady friends by starlight.

A few more houses sat back from the beach, their backyard lights filtering onto the sand.

The Jackson home, then Ms. O'Connor's place.

Matt stopped and leaned out the window as Jason pulled up next to him. "See anything?"

"No, sir. Not a soul from the marina south."

"Mrs. Davenport heard something when she was coming home from her bridge party."

The kid pretended to heft a glass to his lips. "You know those ladies like their wine."

"Those *ladies* are funding your paycheck, young man. Best not disparage the hand that feeds you."

Jason cleared his throat and straightened himself in his seat. "I'll continue south till the cove ends, then backtrack to the marina. Sam needs help with his boat. Won't take long."

"Sullivan on the gate?"

"Roger that. Talked to him a couple minutes ago. Everything's quiet at his end."

"Let me know if you spot anything."

"Will do."

Jason drove on, leaving Matt to stare into the darkness for a long moment before he eased the truck forward.

A flash caught his eye.

He jammed on the brake and studied the night. Ms. O'Connor's house sat shadowed in the distance.

What had he seen? A reflection?

Matt grabbed his keys from the ignition and stepped from his truck.

Probably nothing, but better safe than sorry.

He climbed the trail that led to the property, the sand soft under his feet. Sweat trickled down the small of his back. He wiped at his shirt, then rubbed his left hand across his brow.

Nearing the house, he noted the blinds and draperies were drawn. The house appeared to be locked up tight. For all he knew, Lydia and Tyler could have driven into the mainland for dinner and a late movie.

Something rustled in the wind. He turned toward the sound. Saw movement. An animal. No—

A man.

Standing on a picnic table, he was peering through the small window.

Matt charged the deck.

The guy turned, his face backlit.

Tall, medium build.

Dark shirt, khaki pants, baseball cap. The guy leaped down and dashed out of sight.

Hoisting himself over the railing, Matt followed him around the side of the house, then stopped short in the front yard.

The Peeping Tom had disappeared.

Dense forest surrounded the landscaped lawn. A path cut through the underbrush. Matt raced forward, dodging branches and pushing back the thick foliage.

The trail led to the property next door.

Rob Jackson stood on his deck, pointing. "Kid headed for the beach. About a minute ahead of you."

"Which way did he turn?"

"North. Toward the marina."

Matt raced to the beach and scanned the shoreline. Nothing moved in either direction.

Grabbing his radio, he punched in the dispatcher's code. "Eunice, Peeping Tom at 50 Cove Road. Have Jason backtrack to the O'Connor house. Alert Sullivan. We're looking for a Caucasian male, tall, medium build, dark shirt, khaki trousers, cap. Contact me if they see anyone who fits that description."

Matt ran north along the beach until Jason pulled up beside him.

"Jackson saw the kid," Matt explained. "Ran through his yard, turned north."

"Probably one of those punks from the mainland."

Matt nodded. "Follow the beach to the marina, then do a sweep of the island. I'll head out along Cove Road soon as I check on Ms. O'Connor's houseguest."

Matt followed the path to the O'Connor property, circled the house and climbed the stairs to the front porch.

He knocked twice. "Lydia, it's Matt."

She inched the door open. The look on her face told Matt she was anything but pleased to see him.

"How dare you look through the sitting room window." Her eyes were wide with accusation. "You're depraved. Sick."

He held up his hands in defense. "You've got the wrong guy."

"I *saw* you running away. Same shirt, cap. You're always snooping around. Last time you had your gun drawn. Now you're looking in my window."

"Lydia, you saw a Peeping Tom."

She laughed ruefully. "What? You just happened to be walking by and spied the guy?"

"I wasn't walking by. I was checking your house. Mrs. Davenport heard noise on the beach. I came over to make sure you and Tyler were okay."

Lydia looked as if she was trying to shift gears and couldn't make the transition.

"If it wasn't you," she said, a line of confusion crossing her brow. "Who was it?"

"Probably a mainland teen. It happens occasionally. We'll catch him."

Lydia glanced down at her bare feet and ran a hand through her hair before she looked back at him.

"I'm sorry. I jumped to the wrong conclusion. It's just…I thought Sanctuary would be a safe place to live."

His heart went out to her. She looked frightened, alone. As if she were carrying the weight of the world upon her slender shoulders. And without a soul to help her.

"Why don't you make sure all the doors and windows are locked before I leave? I'll wait on the porch."

Lydia did as he asked and in a few minutes she

returned, stepped out into the night and stood just inches from him. He could smell her perfume. The breeze caught the scent, teasing him as it wafted past.

"Tyler's asleep," she said. "Doors and windows locked."

A few strands of hair fell over her cheek. He wanted to reach out and tuck them back into place.

She stared up into his eyes and moved her lips as if she wanted to tell him something. Was she weighing her options and trying to decide if she could trust him?

He must have lost the toss.

She straightened her shoulders and shoved her jaw forward with determination. "We'll be just fine."

The magic of the moment evaporated into the steamy night. He took a step back. Lydia Sloan wouldn't divulge any secrets to him, at least not this evening.

He could take a hint. Time to leave the woman alone.

"Lock your doors and don't open them to anyone." Matt heard the briskness in his own voice. "And turn on the alarm. Remember the secret code in case you need help." She looked so inviting. He softened for a moment. "I can be here at a moment's notice."

She nodded. "I've got it." She held out her hand.

Matt took it, wishing he could wrap her protectively in his arms. A tingle of electricity tickled his palm, and he held the embrace for longer than necessary.

Then he turned on his heels and headed toward his

pickup. No reason to stay where he wasn't wanted. Two weeks and he'd say goodbye for good.

But before he left, he'd find out what had brought Lydia Sloan to Sanctuary.

EIGHT

After lunch on Saturday, Tyler packed his bag for the sleepover and spent the rest of the day begging Lydia to take him to Bobby's house early.

"Mrs. Jackson said six o'clock, honey. Why don't you read one of your library books while you're waiting."

"Aw, Mom!"

By four o'clock, Lydia was tired of Tyler's whining and sent him to his room for a time-out, while she tried to find something to wear to Joel's party.

She had accepted the invitation to spite Matt. Now, she wished she could stay home with a good book.

When was the last time she'd been to a social gathering, other than a birthday party for one of Tyler's friends? She couldn't remember. Sonny never enjoyed parties. Not that he hadn't gone out in the evening. He called them work-related events, and wives weren't included. Lydia could only imagine the type of work he had been doing.

The phone rang.

"Hello."

"Lydia, it's Katherine. I've decided to extend my stay. Patrick's sister is stronger, but she still needs help. That is if you and Tyler are doing all right without me."

"Of course, we are. Don't worry about us. In fact, I have something planned with the island photographer."

Katherine laughed. "You met Joel?"

"He invited me to his house for a party tonight. Tyler's going to a sleepover at the Jackson home."

"Joel's definitely a ladies' man. He probably decided to give the party just to impress you, dear."

"He seems harmless. Beside, I'm not interested in getting involved with anyone."

"A party would do you good. I bought a couple of dresses on my last shopping trip to New York. But when I brought them home, I realized they're too youthful for a woman my age."

"Now, Katherine, you don't have an old bone in your body." From her chuckle, Lydia was sure the woman appreciated the compliment.

"Well, then maybe I should say, they're not my style. Try them on, Lydia. They've still got the tags on them. See if they fit. I'd be so pleased if you'd get some good out of them. Goodness knows I won't be taking them back. You'll save me from packing them up and giving them to charity."

"You've been too kind already."

"Nonsense. Do me a favor and wear them. I insist."

After hanging up, Lydia opened the closet in the

master bedroom and peered at the clothes hanging neatly on the racks. Just as Katherine had said, Lydia found the dresses, still in plastic garment bags complete with the manufacturers' tags.

Although Lydia knew Katherine would look attractive in anything, the dresses did seem designed with a younger woman in mind. Lydia selected a pale purple sheath. The fit was perfect and the color enhanced her skin tones.

She gasped when she looked at the price tag and promised she would somehow make it up to Katherine. After applying makeup and using a curling iron to add a little bounce to her hair, she returned to the living room.

"Time to go," she called. "Tyler?"

Where was he?

Tyler pulled open the sliding deck door and stepped inside. "I had to get my Frisbee."

"Lock the door, honey." Lydia dashed back to the bedroom to get her purse before she and Tyler hustled out the front door.

"Remember to say 'please' and 'thank you.' And go to bed when Mrs. Jackson tells you to." Climbing into the SUV, she added, "I'll give Mrs. Jackson the telephone number of where I'll be. Call me if you get lonesome."

"Bobby said his mom bought lots of junk food."

Great, Lydia thought. Ever since Sonny's death, Tyler's stomach had bothered him. Nerves, the pediatrician told her. An overload of sweets wouldn't help. Tyler would probably come home exhausted and on a sugar high.

"I brought my Action-Pac, Mom. I told the guys I'd let them use it."

She knew how much the electronic game meant to him. "That would have made Dad happy."

Turning into the Jackson's driveway, Lydia braked to a stop in front of the house. Tall potted palms waved a welcome from the wraparound porch decorated with white wicker furniture.

Tyler stretched out his arms to Lydia. She kissed his cheek and felt a moment of panic slip over her. If anything ever happened to Tyler…

Before she could worry further, he opened the car door and headed toward the house.

Sarah Jackson welcomed them both with a warm smile as she invited them inside. "We're so glad Tyler could be part of the fun."

The home was tastefully decorated but very livable. A couch, love seat and two overstuffed chairs with matching ottomans were attractively arranged around a large brick fireplace. A scattering of toys gave evidence this was a house even kids could enjoy.

Bobby and Chase raced in from the kitchen. "Hey, Tyler. Put your stuff in my room," Bobby said. "Dad's grilling our dinner. Mom baked a cake for dessert."

Rob stuck his head through the kitchen doorway. "Good to see you again, Lydia. Hey, Tyler. Make yourself at home. Dinner in ten minutes. Care to join us, Lydia?"

She shook her head, appreciating the offer. "Thanks, but I'm going out for the evening." She gave Joel's address and phone number to Sarah. "Don't hesitate to call, if there's a problem."

"There won't be," Sarah insisted. "Enjoy the night. You can pick up Tyler about noon."

Her son raced upstairs, then turned back long enough to wave goodbye. Lydia's heart felt a tug. Her little guy was growing up too fast. She was grateful Tyler had found friends and appeared to have forgotten—at least for the moment—all that had happened in Atlanta.

The Jacksons seemed like a great family, committed to kids. Tyler would have a wonderful time at the sleepover.

Lydia needed to find out more about the photo, but maybe she would have some fun tonight, as well.

Then she thought of all that had happened over the last seven months, and she knew she was asking for too much, too soon.

Cars lined the driveway to Joel's expansive beach house. A stone walkway led to the stately entrance where a contemporary crystal chandelier, hanging in the foyer, shimmered through the etched-glass double doors.

Lydia parked her SUV and ran her hand over her stomach, trying to still the butterflies that fluttered there. Heading back to the seclusion of Katherine's home sounded like a good idea at the moment.

Before she could retreat, the front doors opened and Joel waved a greeting. Attempting to smile, she pulled her keys from the ignition and headed for the house.

"You look ravishing," Joel gushed. He hugged her ever so briefly and kissed her turned cheek, then motioned her inside.

An eclectic assortment of leather couches, chrome tables and textured animal-print furnishings filled the great room. On the far wall, a stacked-stone fireplace stretched to meet the crown molding and twelve-foot ceiling. Rattan fans circled lazily overhead while track lighting accentuated a group of muted watercolors and various collections of black-and-white prints.

Jazz played in the background and a mix of twenty- and thirty-somethings, many dressed in sleek black outfits, milled around the great room, sipping red wine.

Joel placed his hand on the small of her back and ushered her forward, dropping the names of those they passed along the way.

Everyone seemed friendly, but when Joel went to check on the hors d'oeuvres, Lydia found herself wondering how soon she could see the photo and head home.

A woman with shoulder-length raven hair and diamond-stud earrings approached. "Joel said you're new to the island."

"Actually, I'm visiting. Do you live here?" Lydia asked.

The woman shrugged. "Only when Joel invites me to stay. I'm from Jacksonville." She turned and acknowledged the others. "We all are. Joel left there about a year ago. We worked together and hated to see him go. Now, whenever he snaps his fingers and says 'party,' we arrive in a flash."

"Were you with the same law firm?"

The woman tilted head. "What?"

"I thought Joel was a lawyer."

The woman laughed. "Sure, he is."

"Now, Cynthia." Joel appeared from nowhere. "You're not telling stories, are you?" He handed Lydia the soda she requested as Cynthia moved to another circle of friends.

"To new relationships." He raised his wineglass, took a large gulp and wiped his tongue over his lips. "Tell me how you've been entertaining yourself since we last talked."

Lydia doubted Joel would be interested in knowing she walked the floors most nights, wondering what her husband had been involved in that had caused his death. Nor would he care that she was beginning to breathe without feeling tightness in her chest.

She finally decided on a noncommittal response. "Actually, Tyler keeps me busy."

Joel pulled his glass to his lips again, his eyes flickering over his guests. "He's very much the active one, isn't he now?"

Smiling, he waved to someone who had just entered the room. Turning back to Lydia, he bowed. "If you'll excuse me, madame, duty requires me to greet my guest."

"But, what about the photo?"

"Photo? Ah, yes. Give me a minute, would you?" He walked away, leaving her standing alone in the center of the room.

Lydia turned to look out the French doors that opened onto the deck. A few of the guests reclined in sculptured chaise lounges, while others pulled chairs around a teak table decorated with wrought iron hurricane lamps that flickered in the evening breeze. Beyond the Olympic-size pool and landscaped lawn, the deserted beach and placid sea stretched toward the horizon.

More people arrived, and the chatter of the guests soon filled the house. Someone turned up the music's volume. The noise level increased as people talked over the jazz medley.

Lydia put down her glass and walked to a built-in bookshelf where Joel's photographs were displayed. The sooner she found the picture of Sonny, the sooner she'd be able to leave the large and noisy gathering. She yearned to be back at Katherine's—the house that was beginning to feel like home.

She scanned the framed photos. A snapshot of Joel at a poolside barbecue surrounded by bikini-clad women. A party at his house and another shot of his sailboat.

Lydia's heart caught in her throat.

A four-by-six copy of the gull photo sat on the shelf. In the background, one face stood out.

The man *had* to be her husband.

Yet, Sonny had refused to visit Katherine once she moved to Sanctuary. So what was he doing on the island?

Lydia turned as the host approached.

"Contrary to popular opinion, I do not invite attractive women to my parties and then leave them to fend for themselves," Joel said. "And I certainly don't introduce them to other eligible bachelors who might edge me out of consideration."

Lydia forced a smile. "You have a beautiful home, Joel."

He shrugged. "Only as beautiful as the people who fill it." He placed his glass on the bookshelf and reached for her free hand. "Lydia, I haven't been able to get you off my mind since that day we met on the beach."

"Joel—"

"I understand you and your son are here for a vacation. I'm hoping that includes getting to know me better. I'd love to take you sailing. Perhaps candlelight dinners when Tyler stays at his friend's house."

Her pulse raced but not with attraction. Joel had acquired a slight lisp, no doubt from the wine he had consumed.

Someone opened the doors that led to the deck. A stiff breeze blew through the house, causing her to shiver.

"You're cold." Joel released her hand and draped his arm over her shoulders. "Let me keep you warm."

Lydia pointed to the photo on the shelf and tried

to edge out of his embrace. "Tell me about this picture, Joel. When was it taken?"

Her host shrugged. "In the past year or so."

"This man," Lydia indicated Sonny "do you know him?"

He squinted at the photo. "Maybe a visitor to the island. Or someone's houseguest. I can't place him to tell you the truth."

Truth? That's what Lydia was seeking.

The doorbell rang, the sound barely audible above the music. If only Joel would stay put and not rush off to welcome the newcomer. She needed to learn more about the photo before he disappeared again.

"Any idea who this other man is?" The second man's face had been cut out of the picture.

"Let me see." Joel bent to take a closer look, his head touching hers.

"What's going on here?" a voice demanded behind Lydia.

She turned. "Matt?"

The security chief stood three feet away.

Joel dropped his arm from around Lydia and swaggered forward. "Who invited *you?*"

"Someone called in a noise complaint, Mr. Cowan. You know the regulations."

"Since when is having a party against the rules?"

"The music's too loud. Lower the volume and there won't be a problem."

"The only problem is a security chief who thinks he's still in Miami." Joel hit his forehead with the palm of his hand. "Now I remember. You turned in your badge, didn't you? Something about not being there to back up your partner?"

Matt's face darkened. A muscle twitched in his jaw. Lydia saw his hands fist as if he was ready to punch the lawyer in the gut.

"Catch that Peeping Tom yet, Lawson?" Joel continued to taunt. "Just exactly what are we paying you for?"

"Turn down the music," Matt said through clenched teeth.

The host eyed a man standing near the sound system and nodded almost imperceptibly. The house fell silent.

Candles flickered, casting shadows into the corners of the room. Matt glanced around at the various groups of people now standing silent.

Joel's arm returned to circle Lydia's shoulders. She tried to step away, but he pulled her closer.

Matt's gaze rested on Lydia. "Everything okay?"

Before she could answer, Joel spoke. "Everything was fine until you barged in. Lydia and I were enjoying a night together." His voice was laced with innuendo.

Lydia shrugged out of Joel's embrace, feeling soiled by his touch. The last thing she wanted was to be in the middle of two men trying to one-up the other. She'd had enough of the party, her slightly intoxicated host and the security chief who seemed to always appear out of thin air.

"The party's over for me, gentlemen. Good night."

Squaring her shoulders, she strode toward the door. Halfway there, she remembered the photo. No way would she turn around and retrace her steps.

She'd talk to Joel another time, when his head was clear and his lips untied and when Matt wasn't around to interfere.

Pulling in a deep breath, she stuck her chin into the air with determination and marched out the front door.

Matt followed Lydia from the house and climbed into his truck just as she turned her SUV onto the main road. He'd handled that with about as much finesse as a mule taking dance lessons. And he'd felt just about as awkward. Not because he'd walked into an upscale home or confronted the host and caused some of the guests an anxious moment. None of that bothered him a hoot.

The real problem was seeing Lydia wrapped in Joel's arms. Just how long had she planned to stay at the party?

Matt turned the key and tramped down on the accelerator. The wheels squealed, leaving a streak of rubber. A little present for Cowan when he worked through his hangover in the morning. He'd be sure to remember who interrupted his plans with Lydia.

The thought of the sleazeball putting the moves on her made Matt burn, literally. He turned the air conditioner to high and adjusted the vent so the cool air blasted over him.

Not that he had any romantic feelings for the

newcomer. She was simply out of her element when it came to the likes of Joel Cowan. Money could turn a girl's head. Money, and a fancy car, a sailboat, a beachside mansion.

"You think you'd learn," Matt growled under his breath.

A pretty face distracted a man, caused him to think irrationally or not at all. And Matt knew too well when a man was distracted, tragic things could happen.

He didn't need a woman in his life. Or so he kept telling himself.

Bottom line, he didn't deserve one, either.

Lydia turned the SUV's air conditioner to high, trying to cool her frustration. Once again Matt Lawson had barged into her life. This time, when she and Joel were talking about the photo of Sonny.

What was the connection between her husband and the lawyer? The Men's Club? Could Joel be involved in the Atlanta operation?

She'd been so close to finding out before Matt had thrown Joel off course.

No one had called in a complaint about the music. Matt told her the lots were five-acre tracts. Music wouldn't travel that far, especially with the pounding surf and ocean breeze as a backdrop. The only one who had been disturbed was the security chief.

The look on his face continued to float through her mind. How dare he think she was involved with Joel?

She adjusted the air conditioner vent. The cool air

swirled around her, fanning her hair away from her face. She probably looked like a banshee. Call her a wild woman, but she was mad.

Why couldn't something work out for a change? She wasn't any closer to exposing Sonny's killers or finding a way to protect her son.

She forced out a deep breath as sadness overcame her anger. She'd made a mess of her life. Growing up, she'd thought love was forever. She'd asked God to bless her marriage, and trusted He would.

The sting of reality hurt too much.

She and Sonny had done more than drift apart. They had taken giant strides. And it seemed Sonny had taken the largest steps to distance himself. Not that Lydia had minded at the time. When there was nothing left to hold on to, being alone with Tyler outweighed trying to fake a relationship with her husband.

Lydia passed the turnoff to the Jackson's house. More than anything she wanted to see her son, wrap her arms around him and whisper that she loved him. But she was being overprotective again. She needed to give Tyler space to grow. He was safe with the Jacksons. No reason for her to ruin his evening just because hers had turned out so bad.

Katherine's drive loomed ahead. A feeling of dread settled over Lydia. Probably fatigue. A cup of herbal tea would help.

The memory of the face at the window sent a shiver down her spine. This time she'd make sure the curtain was completely closed.

Pulling into the driveway, she shook her head at her own stupidity. She'd left before dark and hadn't turned on the porch light or left a lamp burning inside. Nervous about the party, she'd rushed out the door without thinking.

Now, the house sat dark and empty.

The trees rustled an ominous greeting as she stepped from the car.

Silly goose. Always afraid of the night.

Mustering her courage, she walked defiantly to the front door, clicking her heels hard against the concrete.

For all her determination, fear wrapped its ugly hand around her. Shaking off her trepidation, she turned the key in the lock. The door swung open.

Silence.

Goose bumps rose on her arms.

Her neck tingled a warning. She thought she'd turned on the alarm.

Her hand groped for the wall switch. Light filled the room. She blinked.

The pillows on the couch were exactly as she had left them. The newspaper sat folded on the coffee table next to the chapter book Tyler was reading.

Her eyes glanced into the corner by the couch. Tyler's book bag had been zipped up and tucked under the side table when they had left the house. Now it lay open, papers and pencils scattered around the floor.

Tyler didn't have a key so he couldn't have come home.

Lydia reached for the security alarm and punched in the silent emergency alarm.

She needed help.

Someone had been in the house.

NINE

Lydia sat in her SUV with the engine running, waiting for her call for help to be answered. She eyed the house. If anyone was still inside and tried to run, she'd floor the accelerator and escape down the drive.

She rubbed her hands over her arms. The heat of her earlier anger had turned to bone-chilling cold. Her skin crawled as if a thousand bugs were swarming over her flesh.

What would an intruder want with Tyler's book bag?

Headlights illuminated the driveway. She recognized Matt's pickup.

"Someone broke in while I was gone," she called, as he jumped from his truck, gun in hand, and raced toward the front door.

"Stay outside, Lydia. I'll tell you when it's clear."

She followed him up the steps and waited at the door while he searched the main living areas before heading down the hall to the bedrooms. Returning to the great room, he approached the sliding-glass door that led to the deck and tugged on the handle. The door slid open.

Lydia's heart thumped hard against her chest. "Tyler went outside before we left the house. He must have forgotten to slip the lock in place."

Matt closed the door, engaged the lock and bent to latch the special anti-intrusion device Katherine had installed.

Pulling the draperies across the large panes of glass, he blocked out their view of the night and anyone else's view into the house.

"Any idea what's been stolen?" he asked.

She stepped inside. "I haven't looked around. When I opened the door, I saw Tyler's book bag and was afraid to go any farther."

The puzzled look on his face made her backtrack. She told him about the school supplies scattered on the floor, and her immediate concern someone had broken in.

"Let's check Katherine's high-value items," Matt suggested.

The sterling flatware and serving pieces were in neat rows in the silver chest. A collection of figurines sat untouched on the curio shelves and the oil painting of Christ in the boat with the disciples still hung on the wall. Even the few pieces of jewelry Katherine had left behind seemed to be in their original spots. As far as Lydia could tell, nothing had been taken.

"Maybe Tyler came home to get something. Why

don't you call the Jacksons? Just say you want to tell Tyler good-night."

Lydia dialed the number.

Rob answered. "The guys are already in their pajamas and watching a movie. Want to talk to him?"

"If you don't mind. You know mothers, we like to check on our sons."

"Hey, not a problem. Sarah's the same way. I understand completely."

"Do I have to come home?" Tyler complained when he got on the phone.

"No, honey. I just wanted to know if you were having a good time."

"The greatest. Mrs. Jackson made chocolate cake. She let us eat in the living room. Now we're watching a movie. Mr. Jackson said he'd pop popcorn."

"Did you go outside tonight?"

"Just to eat dinner. Mrs. Jackson said we could have a cookout on the deck. We roasted marshmallows on the barbecue. Then we came inside for cake."

"And you didn't come home for anything?"

"I don't have a key, Mom."

"What about earlier, Tyler? You went out to get your Frisbee. Do you remember locking the sliding door?"

Tyler sighed. "I don't remember."

"Okay, honey. You better get back to the movie. Have a good night. And get some sleep."

He hesitated. "Mom, you'll come and get me tomorrow, won't you?"

"Mrs. Jackson said the party would be over at noon. I'll see you then."

She hung up and looked at Matt. "Tyler never left their deck."

Matt nodded and glanced around the room. "I'll make a note of the incident so it's on record, but there's nothing more I can do."

"Shouldn't the police be notified?"

"The mainland cops rely on my folks to patrol the island. I call them in when there's a crime, but..." He paused for a moment. "I have to tell you, Lydia, an open book bag doesn't prove someone's been in the house."

She didn't know whether to be angry or relieved but settled on the latter.

"Maybe I'm blowing this whole thing out of proportion." She tried to go back over the day's activities. "Tyler's book bag was under the table. I turned on the alarm before I left. The sliding doors were locked, but Tyler went back outside."

"Even if they were unlocked, the alarm would have tripped if someone opened the door. Who else has the code?" he asked.

"No one I know of." She dug her fingers through her hair and sighed. "Surely Katherine wouldn't have given it to anyone."

"I agree. It doesn't sound like something she'd do." He gave the room another look, then stepped toward the door. "Well...it's time for me to head out."

Lydia didn't want to be alone just yet. "How about a cup of coffee? Decaf okay?"

He hesitated a moment, then nodded. "Sounds great."

In the kitchen, she placed the ground coffee beans in the basket and poured water into the reservoir. A rich aroma soon filled the air.

"Guess I spoiled the party for you tonight," Matt said.

Lydia shrugged. "You told me earlier that you didn't like Joel."

"Yeah? Well, I should keep my opinions to myself." He turned away from her and looked out the window. "I keep thinking he might be involved in more than he lets on."

After seeing the photo of Sonny, she was beginning to agree. She leaned against the counter and watched Matt pull out a chair and sit at the kitchen table.

"You were a policeman in Miami?" she prodded.

He nodded. "Yeah. Detective."

"And something happened to your partner? Is that what Joel was referring to?"

Matt wiped an imaginary speck of dust from the top of the table. "Look, Lydia, I'd rather not discuss it."

She turned her back on him and opened the cabinet. So he didn't want to talk. She knew how that felt. Some things were too painful to share.

She placed two mugs on the counter. "Cream or sugar?"

He shook his head. "Black."

"Talking helps." The words surprised even her.

"Then tell me something about Lydia Sloan," he said, his gaze steady yet warm.

She poured the coffee, carried the cups to the table and sat next to him. "What's to tell? Married, one child, husband deceased."

"And you left Atlanta—"

"I told you. Katherine invited us here for a little vacation." She raised the cup to her lips and took a sip. "Is this déjà vu of the night we met?"

He toyed with his mug. "The night you blew in on the heels of a storm."

She laughed. "Now that sounds sinister."

He raised an eyebrow and stared at her.

"I thought we were discussing *your* past," she said in self-defense.

"Cowan talks too much, and you, Miss Newcomer, don't talk enough."

She ignored his comment. "Why *did* you leave Miami, Matt?"

"Got tired of the big city, wanted a little peace and quiet."

"Hmm. My take is something happened to your partner. You feel responsible."

"Now you're psychic?"

"Just reading the signals you send."

"And your signals?" he asked.

She tilted her head and shrugged. "Don't have any. I'm the proverbial open book. Married the first guy I dated. Wanted to get away from a bad home life and ended up in another." She tried to smile.

"Sometimes I wonder what makes the difference."

She wrinkled her brow. "Difference?"

"Why some marriages work and others don't," he said.

"I asked Katherine that very question once when her husband was so sick. 'Trust in God,' she told me." Lydia shook her head, sadness sweeping over her again. "After he died, I didn't know how her faith could stay so strong."

Matt pursed his lips. "Sounds like my partner's wife. My selfishness cost her a lifetime of grief. Yet she forgave me."

Lydia looked into his eyes and saw the pain he tried to keep buried.

"Deep down I know God forgives me," Matt said. "I'm just not sure I can forgive myself."

Forgiveness. Trust. Big issues Lydia wasn't ready to face. She pushed back on the chair and stood. "More coffee?"

He cleared his throat, wiped a hand over his chin. "Yeah. Thanks."

She refilled his cup, returned the pot to the counter, then glanced through the windows to the darkness outside.

Suddenly her courage faltered.

Tears burned her eyes. She blinked to control their onslaught.

She was being paranoid. No one knew she was in Sanctuary. Tyler was safe with the Jacksons. After Matt left, she'd lock the doors and turn on the alarm.

Of course, she wouldn't sleep and the lights would burn until dawn.

Matt rose and touched her arm. "What's wrong?"

A stream of tears rolled down her cheeks. "I'm tired of being afraid."

TEN

"Talk to me, Lydia."

The warmth in Matt's voice touched her. She gazed into his eyes and saw something she hadn't seen before—compassion, concern, even a little empathy.

"What happened in Atlanta?" he asked.

"There…there was a fire." Whether it was the late hour or the haunting memory, the words slipped out before she realized.

Then she shrugged, wiped her hand over her damp face, trying to bolster her courage. "Look, it's past. Tyler and I are making a new life for ourselves."

"You told me talking helps."

She shook her head. "There's nothing to talk about."

"What about your husband?"

She didn't want to think about the fire. But the panic she had felt that night returned. Her palms grew damp. She wiped them on her dress.

"I got Tyler outside and started to go back for Sonny. One of the firemen stopped me. I struggled with him, wanted to keep going, but there was no hope."

Matt reached out and stroked her cheek. A tender gesture.

A lump filled her throat. She swallowed, willing her voice to work. "Sonny and I didn't have the best marriage. But I never wanted anything to happen to him."

"Were you leaving him, Lydia?"

More tears spilled over her lashes. She nodded. "Tyler and I were moving out in the morning."

Matt stepped closer and wrapped his arm around her shoulders. She dropped her head onto his chest and let the tears fall. She cried for her husband who had died, for her son exposed to too much pain and for a way of life that had been replaced with fear.

Someone had wanted Sonny dead. She had tried to learn the truth while she was in Atlanta, but every path led to a dead end. Now she was hiding out on a remote island, hoping the people who had killed Sonny wouldn't find her or Tyler.

And for some reason, she had turned to a former cop who might have connections with the police in Atlanta. Don't trust him, an inner voice whispered. Yet tonight, she was ignoring that warning.

Matt wrapped Lydia in his arms. The woman's heart was broken, and she was grieving for everything that had happened to her and to her child.

"Shh. It's going to be okay, Lydia."

She was soft and slender, a mere wisp of a woman but with a backbone strong as rawhide. Most of all, he admired her courage. She'd left everything behind in Atlanta and had come to this secluded spot. But why? Was it merely to get away from the pain? From the strength of her sobs, it appeared she had carried the pain with her.

She was running from something—perhaps the police's attempt to blame her for Sonny's death. They didn't have any evidence or they would put out an APB for her arrest.

What had her husband been involved in? A man could get himself into a heap of trouble. No reason why a woman and child had to be hurt because of it.

"There, there, Lydia. You're safe with me. I won't let anything happen to you."

She sniffed.

He reached for a box of tissues on the counter. "Dry your eyes."

She grabbed a tissue, wiped it over her cheeks and blew her nose. When she glanced up at him her eyes were red and her face splotched, but she looked more beautiful than any woman he had ever known.

"That's better," he said as she forced a smile.

He hugged her briefly before she pulled from his embrace and walked to the sink.

"I usually don't cry." She splashed water on her face and wiped it dry with a paper towel.

"You don't have to be so strong, Lydia."

"I never want Tyler to see—"

"You want to protect him. I know. But you need to work through your fear."

"Like you're doing with your guilt?"

He shook his head. "Guess we're broken in different ways."

"At least you can turn to God for help," she said. "Trust Him, Lydia."

Her eyes narrowed. "That's the problem, I can't trust anyone."

Lydia punched her pillow, hoping to get comfortable. The bed in Katherine's master bedroom seemed bigger than usual. And lonelier.

She had eventually told Matt to go home. She'd be fine. But as much as she wanted to push her fears aside, the possible break-in had made her resolve crumble like blue cheese. Left alone, she wouldn't have closed her eyes all night.

And Matt knew it. He had volunteered to spend the night out front in his pickup. Asked for a bottle of water. Nothing else.

She had padded to bed, hoping to sleep off her anxiety. Now, hours later, her eyes were still wide-open. Sleep seemed to elude her, no matter who was guarding the house.

She rolled to her left side and forced her eyes shut. Two seconds later, they flew open as a vision of Matt flashed through her mind. He was scrunched up in the driver's seat, legs jammed against the dashboard, his arms wrapped around his chest. She moaned and tried to focus on something else.

Tyler.

She smiled, thinking of the stories he'd tell when she picked him up in the morning. He would square his slender shoulders, attempting to look grown-up as he talked about the sleepover.

Her mind backtracked to before the fire, before Sonny's death. Tyler had been a happy-go-lucky little boy who loved life.

Of course, all that had changed.

Her eyes closed, she saw the flames, smelled the smoke. Tonight, it seemed so real.

Pulling herself from the bed, she reached for a bathrobe and slipped it on before she glanced at the clock—2:00 a.m.

Accustomed to the dark, she walked resolutely out of the bedroom and down the hallway, stopping at the front window to peer outside. Matt's pickup was parked in the driveway.

Good to his word, she saw the shadow of his body lodged in the driver's seat.

In their years of marriage, Sonny had never sacrificed his comfort for hers. Matt had his own battles to fight, but he was sleeping in the truck to protect her.

She wanted to believe Matt was a good guy with a big heart. Yet Tyler's safety depended on her being cautious.

The first light of dawn warmed the horizon as Matt crawled out of his pickup and stretched. He'd spent the last few hours thinking of Lydia and how good she'd felt in his arms.

He looked toward the heavens.

Lord, I don't deserve Your mercy. But Lydia's hurting. She needs You in her life. Help her to find her way. And if I can, let me be Your instrument.

Morning prayer offered, he walked around the house, checked that the doors were locked and scanned the perimeter of the yard, ensuring no one hovered nearby.

A home, a wife, a child—

Was that what he wanted?

With only an efficiency apartment attached to security headquarters and a pickup to call his own, he wasn't what women were looking for in the husband line. He shook his head. No reason to think Lydia would be different from any other woman.

A cool morning breeze followed him as he walked back to his truck. He climbed in, then turned to stare at the silent house.

What is it about you, Lydia? Suddenly, I'm yearning for something more in my life. And that scares me.

He put the gear into Reverse and backed down the drive. He'd better leave Sanctuary before his heart overruled his head.

Lydia heard Matt's truck pull out of the drive. In a way, she felt relieved. Just knowing he had been outside had kept her pulse racing and her mind on anything but sleep.

Once again, she slipped from the bed and stepped into the hallway. Stillness surrounded her as she walked to the window, pulled back the curtain and watched his pickup turn onto Cove Road, heading south.

Last night she'd broken down in Matt's arms and allowed him to see her vulnerability. From here on, she needed to be strong.

Crawling back into bed, she closed her eyes. An image of Matt, holding her in his arms, drifted through her mind as she fell asleep.

The phone jarred her awake a few hours later. She reached for the receiver and wiped a hand over her eyes, trying to clear her vision and her brain. The clock read 8:00 a.m.

"Lydia, it's Joel."

The last person she wanted to hear from this morning.

"Look, I'm really sorry about last night," he said. "You were a jewel to face a roomful of strangers. And then I was tied up with host duties."

Joel had been the problem, not the strangers.

"When Lawson barged in…well, I reacted."

"You guys always seem to butt heads."

"He's a jerk."

"Joel!"

"Okay. Guess he was doing his job or so he said. Still…" Joel paused. "I'm sorry our sparring made you uncomfortable."

"Apology accepted."

"Let me make it up to you over breakfast. There's a coffee shop at the marina. Coffee and sweet rolls perhaps? Afterward, we could take my boat out for a little spin around the island, if you'd like. Especially since we didn't have enough time to get to know each other last night."

Plenty of time to know she didn't want any more to do with the playboy sailor. But the photo of Sonny flashed through her mind, followed by the strange look Joel's guest had given Lydia when she asked about his law firm.

What was Joel involved in? Did he have ties to Sonny and the Men's club?

Lydia was sure of one thing. She needed to find out more.

"Coffee sounds fine, Joel. I'll skip the boat. Hate to admit it, but I'm afraid of the water. And would you mind bringing that photo I showed you last night?"

"Not a problem. I'll see you at the marina. Say in thirty minutes?"

She hung up, hoping she'd soon know more about Sonny's island visit.

A gentle breeze blew across the marina and played with Lydia's hair as she stepped from her SUV. Pulling the wayward strands from her face, she scanned the rows of luxury crafts and spied Joel in the distance, sitting at a sidewalk table in front of the coffee shop. He waved and stood as she walked toward him.

"Morning, Joel," she said, slipping into the wrought iron chair he held for her. A manila envelope lay on the table.

The sun hung in the eastern sky and warmed

Lydia's face. She glanced at the boats docked nearby, grateful to be on dry ground.

"I ordered two coffees and a basket of pastries," Joel said as a waitress appeared with two filled mugs and an assortment of sweet rolls and muffins.

"Thanks again for the party last night," Lydia said once they were alone.

"Everyone loved meeting you."

"Really? Who was the woman I talked to while you got my soda?"

"Cynthia?"

"That's right. She said you invited her up often."

He smirked as if he had a secret and leaned forward to share it. "Cynthia would like to be invited up on a permanent basis."

"She's very attractive."

He stared at Lydia for a long moment. "But not my type."

Lydia glanced away. Water lapped against the side of the nearby pier. Gulls flew overheard. Perhaps the same birds that flew near her husband the day Joel had snapped his picture.

Lydia pointed to the envelope. "Did you bring the photo?"

"An eight-by-ten. Thought the enlargement might give you more clarity." He pulled the glossy from the envelope.

Lydia stared at the now clearly defined face.

No doubt about it. The man in the photo was her husband.

"Friend of yours?" Joel asked before taking a sip of coffee.

Friend? "He looks like someone I knew in Atlanta."

"Nice town."

"You go there often?" Lydia slanted a glance at Joel.

He shrugged. "Two, three times a year. Take in a Braves game, have a nice dinner in Buckhead, do a little shopping."

"Buckhead, huh?" Where Sonny's club was located. "Ever hear of the Men's Club?"

Joel shook his head. "Sounds like a place where a guy could get into trouble."

Trouble was an understatement. Lydia tried to read his body language. Was he telling the truth or playing her for a fool?

She pointed to Sonny and then the man whose face was cut out of the picture. "Any idea why these guys were on the island?"

"As I recall, they were just passing through. Haven't seen either of them since." Joel bent closer to the photo. He studied the frame, then chuckled. "Only thing I can tell you, the guy out of camera range must like that new action game everyone's talking about."

"What?"

Lydia's eyes flew back to the photo. This time she noticed the man's wrist draped over Sonny's shoulder.

Her stomach roiled. The enlargement clearly showed the man was wearing a watch—an A.P. digital.

The same type of watch the man in the school yard

had worn. Had Sonny been friends with the man who had tried to kidnap their son?

Suddenly, she felt sick. Rubbing her hand over her stomach, she watched as Joel grabbed a sweet roll and took a large bite of the cream-filled pastry.

The island photo bug was as transparent as the negatives he developed. Self-centered and ostentatious, but he was easy to read. And she was sure of one thing. He had told her the truth when he said he didn't know Sonny.

As Joel reached for his coffee, his phone rang. He withdrew the cell from his pocket and looked at the caller ID, then chuckled as he raised it to his ear.

"Cynthia. I thought you'd be in Jacksonville by now." He paused before glancing at his watch. "Fifteen minutes? Sure, meet you at the house."

Closing his cell, he gave Lydia a sheepish grin. "Sorry, but Cynthia forgot her makeup case. I have to run."

Joel pulled his wallet from his hip pocket. "Promise me, we'll do this again. Soon."

Lydia didn't want to commit to anything.

He dropped a few bills on the table. "Next time there will be no interruptions." He winked, then walked to his car and drove away.

Lydia glanced down at the photo of her husband. What had brought Sonny and the other man to Sanctuary? The man with the A.P. digital? The man who had tried to grab Tyler?

Lydia shook her head. Would she ever find all the

pieces to the puzzle? Or would she and Tyler spend the rest of their lives hiding out?

Matt poured himself another cup of coffee and swallowed the bitter brew, wondering how many gallons of high-test he had consumed in the last six hours. He was riding on pure caffeine at this point, but he had a pile of paperwork to catch up on before he called it a day.

Plus, he'd wasted enough time thinking about Lydia, a woman he couldn't have and had no business wanting.

Butch Griffin, the retired cop Harris recommended, called an hour later. Matt wiped a tired hand over his face.

"Yeah, take I-95 south until you hit the turnoff," Matt told Butch over the phone. "We're about an hour and a half from the highway, due east. Bay Road will lead you onto the island. Tell the guard at the gate you've got an appointment with me. He'll direct you to my office."

When Butch walked in a few hours later, he was exactly what Matt expected: middle-aged with an extra twenty pounds tacked on over muscle. He had a no-nonsense look and a propensity to frown.

Matt offered him a seat and an opportunity to explain why he wanted the job.

"Retired from the Atlanta P.D. after twenty years," Butch recounted. "Been working nights for a computer company since then. Watching their equipment, supplies."

Butch sniffed. "Got bored with the routine. Then they downsized. Harris mentioned this job. Sounded like what I've been looking for. Plus, I've got a daughter who lives on the mainland, not far from here. Her mama and me divorced when she was in middle school. Now she's on her own with a kid on the way. Thought being close to family would be good for a change."

Butch's comment about wanting to be part of a family struck home with Matt. He'd been feeling the same way recently.

The retired cop seemed to be the answer to Matt's staff shortage problem. And he trusted Harris's recommendation.

"Basically, we've got a friendly community here on the island," Matt explained. "People take care of themselves and watch out for their property."

Butch nodded. "After Atlanta it looks like a piece a cake."

"We have had a few incidents recently. A Peeping Tom bothered one of the residents. Later, the woman thought someone had entered her home." Matt cleared his throat. "I don't know if there's a tie-in, but you never know."

"I got ya."

"The mainland's had a number of break-ins. The sheriff's handling the investigation." Matt shrugged. "Even sleepy little waterfront communities have their problems."

"Anything else?"

"About a year ago, there was talk a high-level crime operation was seeking to make their headquarters in this area. Nothing's turned up." Matt paused. "Still, keep your eyes open."

Butch wiped a hand over his jaw. "Friend of mine worked in Miami. Said you were one of the best."

Matt nodded his appreciation. "He tell you why I turned in my badge?"

Butch dropped his gaze and cleared his throat. "Not him. But I heard talk."

Information traveled in law enforcement. Griffin had probably asked a few questions. Matt couldn't blame him. Any new hire would want to know as much as possible about the man for whom he was going to work.

Matt let out the deep breath he was holding. "Harris mention it?"

"Naw. Not Harris. He's close-lipped, but one of the other guys. Guess he had a buddy in your old department. Said you weren't to blame for your partner's death."

Matt's stomach tightened. He remembered his cell phone ringing and the message Pete had left on voice mail. *"Drug bust's going down tonight. Meet me at the warehouse."*

A message Matt had retrieved too late.

Butch sniffed again. "A guy can't see around the corners. You know what I mean?"

Matt knew all too well what Butch meant. "You've got the job, if you want it."

"Appreciate it."

Matt stuck out his hand. "Take the day to find a place to live. Plenty of rental units on the mainland. You might want to stop by the sheriff's office while you're there, introduce yourself. We work pretty closely with his department. Fact is they allow us a lot of leeway here on the island. We call them in if we've got a serious problem or need to make an arrest. Other than that, they leave us pretty much to fend for ourselves." Matt handed Butch a map of the area. "That's the way I like it."

"Sounds like you and me will do just fine." Butch stood, grabbed the map and drew his hand to his forehead in the form of a salute.

"See you tomorrow, bright and early," Matt said. "We'll get you some clothes. Fill out the paperwork and you'll be good to go."

After Butch left, Matt called the sheriff's office to let them know to expect the new security guard. Eunice would get the forms ready, and by the end of the next workday, Butch would officially be on the payroll.

If the new hire worked out the way Matt hoped, he might be able to leave Sanctuary ahead of schedule.

Picking up the phone, Matt tapped in a Miami number.

"You've reached the voice mail of Detective Don Wilson. To leave a message…"

Matt followed the prompt and waited for the beep. "Don, it's Matt Lawson. Everything's quiet along the Georgia coast. I'm ready to find greener pastures. Let me know if you've heard anything new."

He hung up and reached for his Bible, rubbed his fingers over the soft leather, then flipped through the pages.

Lead me, Lord. Don't let me become complacent or swayed by my heart. Show me the path You would have me walk. Into Your hands, I commend my spirit.

ELEVEN

Twenty-four hours later, Sam Snyder's retirement papers lay on Matt's desk stamped with the Island Association's approval. With Butch Griffin on the job, there was no reason not to let Sam go. Matt enjoyed the old man, liked to hear his banter about the early days on the island and appreciated the knowledge he had gained over the years. But Sam's heart was no longer in security.

Butch seemed to be more than up to filling the old man's shoes. Of course, not all the members of the team were happy about the new hire.

Jason pushed open the door to the security office and stomped across the hardwood floor. He glared at Matt, then grabbed the coffeepot and poured himself a cup.

"What's bugging you?" Matt asked. "Bad grade on one of your finals?"

"As if you don't know."

Matt sighed. "You've been madder than a hornet since Butch Griffin started on the job. He give you a hard time?"

Jason shook his head. "Not me. It's Natalie."

Matt scrunched up his face. For the life of him he couldn't figure out what Jason's long-lost love had to do with the new hire from Atlanta.

"Bet he didn't mention anything about kin of his living in the area," Jason said.

"Matter of fact, he said his daughter had a place over on the mainland."

"And did he tell you her name?"

Matt shook his head. "And I didn't ask."

"Well, it's Natalie. Natalie Baxter. Her mom remarried after she divorced Griffin. Seems Natalie's stepdad adopted her. She took his name, Baxter."

The security group was a tight-knit team—small but committed—with each man knowing he could depend on the others. From the tone of Jason's voice, the young man standing before Matt would have a hard time working with Natalie's biological dad.

"What's the real problem, Jason? You still in love with Natalie?"

Matt knew he'd struck pay dirt by the look on Jason's face. The girl had found greener pastures while the young man served his country in Iraq. Not the first time some deserving "Joe" got the shaft because Uncle Sam deployed him far from home. Matt felt for the kid, but life wasn't easy, a lesson Jason had learned the hard way when he returned home.

Jason sniffed. "Natalie didn't have anything good to say about her dad when we were in high school."

"She was just a teenager." Matt didn't want to defend the new hire against a current one, but Jason seemed ready to blow this whole thing out of proportion.

While Natalie seemed nice enough, her judgment of her father had a lot of bias. Jason wasn't taking that into consideration.

"Whatever happened was a long time ago and it involved Butch and his wife. No need to bring a man's past into the job today. You understand me, Jason?"

The kid stared at Matt for a long minute. "I'll work with him. But if I catch him doing anything to Natalie, I'll—"

"He told me he was trying to reconnect with his daughter. Having her father around might be good when the baby comes."

Matt tried to remember if he'd seen a ring on Natalie's left hand. "Who'd she marry?"

"No one. The guy left the area when he found out she was pregnant."

"That baby will need a man in his or her life. Butch Griffin's timing might be the best thing that could happen. Give him the benefit of the doubt. People make mistakes."

"I'll keep my eye on him," Jason said. "See what turns up. And you'll be the first to hear, if I find anything wrong. That is, if you're still in Sanctuary."

"I'll make sure there's a competent replacement before I move on, Jas."

"Yeah, right." Sarcasm was evident. "They'll probably make Griffin chief."

Was that the real issue? "He's replacing Sam. The Association's still working on my job."

"Let me know when they find someone." The kid didn't look back as he pushed open the door and walked out of the office.

At least Sam Snyder approved of Griffin. Later that afternoon he stopped by Matt's office to say goodbye.

"Nice to know I'm not leaving the team short-handed," the old-timer admitted. "That new boat of mine is a powerhouse. Eats up the water. If you want to go out for a spin or do a little fishing, I'd be honored to have you aboard."

"Thanks for the offer," Matt said. "One of these days, I'll take you up on it."

"You know the number," Sam said. "Call me anytime. Day or night."

Matt hoped to take a few days off before he left Sanctuary for good. Then he thought of Lydia. Why had she come into his life when he was ready to move on?

He told Jason women could get a man into trouble. Maybe he should listen to his own words of wisdom. Might help him when it came to saying goodbye.

The way his heart reacted every time he got close to Lydia was a sure sign he wasn't thinking straight. Lovely Lydia—a little alliteration that pointed to a problem in his life.

Leave her alone, his voice of reason cautioned.

Matt refused to listen.

* * *

The next morning, Matt answered a call from the City of Miami Police Department.

"It's Don Wilson. Sorry for the delay getting back to you."

"Thought you were probably on the road," Matt said.

"New Orleans."

"Let the good times roll, eh?"

"*Mais, oui, monsieur*. Your ears should have been burning."

Matt straightened in his chair. "How's that?"

"Santiago was spotted leaving a hole-in-the-wall joint down on Bourbon Street."

"José Santiago?"

"One and the same. Right-hand man to Ricky Gallegos."

"The guy who killed Pete," Matt said.

"An undercover cop saw Santiago, then lost his trail."

"He could lead us to Gallegos," Matt reminded Wilson.

"Exactly. Everyone's on heightened alert. I got home late last night and plan to head back in a day or two. Ran into Vic Wallace at the airport. Made me wish I'd majored in computer technology instead of criminal justice. Wouldn't have to worry about scum like Gallegos."

"Vic's doing okay?"

"Living the good life with the I.T. firm he started.

Plus, he took a gamble and invested in that Action-Pac craze sweeping the country. Everything the boy touches turns to gold."

"Is he still doing a little computer consulting on the side?"

"Horwitz calls Vic in when we need help. Speaking of the boss, Horwitz wanted you to know your job's still open."

"He said that?"

"I told you before, Matt. No one blames you."

"Do me a favor. Let me know when Santiago pops up again. I want to be there, Don."

Silence.

"Don?"

"Yeah. I owe you one. I'll make it happen. And think about coming back to Miami. Horwitz said he'll keep the slot open for two more weeks."

Matt hung up the phone feeling a sense of euphoria. Spotting Santiago meant Ricky Gallegos couldn't be far away.

New Orleans. Matt shook his head. He'd wasted all these months in Sanctuary following a bogus lead. Maybe it was time to head back to Miami.

The next call was from the mainland sheriff.

"That new security guard's just what we needed," the sheriff said.

Matt settled back in his chair. "How so, Wayne?"

"Gave us a tip. Seems he met a guy down by the wharf. The guy liked the bottle a little too much.

Started talking. 'Course, he had no idea his buddy buying the booze was involved with law enforcement."

"What'd the guy say?"

"Said he liked to look in windows on the island. Spy on the 'rich broads.' His words, not mine."

Matt tried to recall everything that had happened the night he'd chased the Peeping Tom. Rob Jackson had stood on his back deck, pointing toward the beach. *"Kid ran through my yard. Headed toward the water. 'Bout a minute ahead of you,"* Jackson had said.

"How old's the boozer?" Matt asked the sheriff.

"Forty-two, but he's been worn hard. Looks mid-fifties, if not older."

Not a kid, that's for sure. Maybe Jackson didn't get a good look at him. Or maybe Griffin found the wrong guy.

"A couple of my guys pulled surveillance after your man tipped us off," the sheriff continued. "You'll never guess what we caught the boozer buying?"

"A little crack cocaine?"

"You got that right. We locked him up. Says he never broke into anyone's home, but we'll let the lawyers work that out. Give Griffin a pat on the back. He made our job a lot easier."

Matt returned the phone to the receiver. Griffin was proving his competence. Matt should be elated his newest employee had done such a good job, but something bothered him.

Jealousy?

No. Call it his skeptical nature, but he questioned when things seemed too good to be true.

Like Lydia.

Sweet, smart, a loving mother. Too good to be true? He didn't think so.

It was all true, but she'd landed in some kind of trouble. Her dead husband was probably at the center of it.

Matt glanced at his watch. Time to make a drive through the island, check on the homes of absentee owners…like the one on Cove Road whose owner was in Ireland.

Or maybe it was better he stayed away. No sense tempting fate, and that's what Lydia was—so very tempting.

Lydia left the sliding door open, inviting the ocean breeze and the sounds of Tyler and Bobby Jackson playing on the deck to float through the house. Her heart warmed, and for a brief moment she thought how good it would be to live on the island and call Sanctuary home.

She glanced at the painting hanging on the wall of Christ in the boat with the disciples. Her life had been stormy ever since the fire.

"Jesus, I trust in You." The short prayer stitched on Katherine's sampler came to mind. Call her a doubting Thomas, but Lydia was convinced God didn't listen to her prayers. And if she couldn't rely on God, she had to rely on herself.

A whole world of problems still waited to be solved back in Atlanta. She needed to contact Ruby and the reporter and see if either of them had found information that would shed light on this whole sordid mess.

As soon as Katherine came home to watch Tyler, Lydia would return to Atlanta. With Tyler safe, she could take some risks. If she dug deep enough, the pieces of the puzzle surrounding Sonny's death eventually had to fall into place.

The sound of tires on asphalt drew her attention to the front window as Matt braked his pickup to a stop. She had wanted to call him over the last few days, but what would she say? Funny thing happened the other night. My emotions got the best of me.

Better to let sleeping dogs lie, not that the man stepping across Katherine's porch reminded her of a dog.

Anything but.

She smiled, enjoying the way his broad shoulders filled out his polo shirt. The serious look on his face softened when she threw open the door and laughed.

"I thought about tripping my security alarm so I could see you again."

A smile played over his lips and lit a small glow in the pit of her stomach.

"How about a cool drink on a warm afternoon?" she asked.

"That's the best offer I've had all day." He

stepped into the house as Bobby and Tyler rushed in from the deck.

"Hey, Chief!" Tyler called out.

"What's up, guys?" Matt followed Lydia into the kitchen. The boys scampered after him.

"Bobby said you're the best swimmer around," Tyler said.

Lydia started to squeeze lemons at the counter while Matt motioned the guys to the kitchen window. "Look out there, fellows. What do you see?"

Bobby shrugged. "Water."

"And some big rocks," Tyler added.

"That's right. Rocks and water. But what you don't see is the strong current that can pull you out to sea or throw you up on those boulders. You boys remember what I said about not swimming in this area."

Bobby nodded. "Some of the older guys say they swim there."

"Well, they shouldn't. It's dangerous. And I hope you boys understand good water safety."

"I do, Chief," Bobby said. "But Tyler can't swim. He doesn't know water safety."

Tyler's eyes widened. "Someday I'll take lessons and learn how to swim for miles."

"The chief taught Chase how to swim," Bobby volunteered.

Lydia appreciated Matt's firm yet gentle manner with the two boys. Sonny had little patience with his son and no time for any of his friends. Although she didn't care for talk about rip currents and treacherous rocks, she liked the way Matt was responding to the boys' comments.

"Could you teach me?" Tyler asked.

The sincere look on her son's face made Lydia realize how much her fear was costing Tyler.

"Go outside, boys," she said, hoping to change the subject. "I'll bring you a snack."

Lydia poured four glasses of lemonade arranged them on a tray and carried them to the deck along with a plate of oatmeal cookies."

The boys ate at the picnic table while she and Matt sat nearby.

"You know how to spoil a guy," Matt said, reaching for a cookie. "Smells wonderful."

"Probably just like your mother used to make."

His face clouded, and he shook his head. "There were five of us. More than she could handle. Not that we were bad kids, just rambunctious. Most days, we were lucky to get something to eat for dinner, let alone a snack."

Lydia looked at Tyler and thought about the differences in people's lives. She'd do anything to make her son's childhood one he would always remember with love. At least that's what she hoped.

"Mom tried to provide what we needed," Matt continued. "But times were tough."

"How'd you learn to swim?" she asked.

He smiled. "Church camp each summer. And some great folks who were determined to make a positive impact on my life."

"Swimming lessons and a little spirituality on the side?"

"Made me realize there was more to life than what the gangs at school were telling me. The swimming paid off with a scholarship to college."

"And you could teach Tyler?"

Matt tilted his head and stared at her. "Is that something you *want* me to do?"

The boys suddenly quieted, and Lydia realized Tyler had heard her last question. If the conversation continued, there would be no turning back. But she couldn't let her own concerns affect her son.

She looked at Tyler. His eyes were wide with anticipation.

"Would you teach Tyler to swim?" she asked Matt.

Her son held his breath.

"I'll be out of town for a day or two. But I'd be happy to teach him when I get back."

"Ya-hoo!" Tyler raised his arms over his head and shook them in the air. He slid off the picnic bench and ran to his mother.

"Thanks, Mom." He wrapped his arms around her neck and gave her the biggest bear hug she'd had in months.

She laughed in spite of the anxiety that pricked at her. "Thank Chief Lawson."

Tyler pulled away from her and dashed to hug Matt. "Thank you, thank you, thank you," he said as he buried his head in Matt's chest.

Lydia watched Matt's face soften. He placed his

large hand around the boy and hugged him back. "Don't you worry, before long, you'll be the best swimmer on the whole island."

Lydia hoped she'd never regret her decision to let Tyler learn to swim. She feared the water, feared it for her son as well as herself.

She looked up to the heavens.

If You're listening, God, be forewarned. I'll never forgive You if something happens to Tyler.

Matt drove to Jacksonville, parked in long-term and headed for the terminal. Don Wilson had called earlier from New Orleans. Santiago was holed up in a hotel on St. Ann Street.

The flight took ninety minutes and seemed like an eternity. After all these months of tracking down tips that led no place, Matt wanted to be present when Santiago was captured. Hopefully, he'd lead them to Gallegos.

The flight was uneventful, but deplaning took longer than normal. A woman with three small children struggled with her overhead luggage until Matt came to her aid. He ended up escorting a crying toddler and two young boys off the plane while the mom chattered nonstop that he was an answer to her prayer for help. The family surrounded him through baggage claim and stayed glued to him until he settled them into a cab headed for their Slidell destination.

He'd lost fifteen minutes, max, but this wasn't the

day to play the Good Samaritan. He grabbed a cab, determined to let nothing else sidetrack him.

"French Quarter. St. Ann Street."

Opening his cell phone, he punched in Wilson's number.

"I'm heading your way. Give me thirty minutes," Matt said when the detective answered.

"We'll have Santiago in custody by then," Wilson promised.

Matt clicked the phone shut. The hunt for Pete's killer was almost over. Santiago would talk and tell them where to find Gallegos. More than anything, Matt wanted to call Connie and tell her he'd found her husband's killer. He owed her that much.

Maybe then, he'd be able to face Enrico.

Matt shook his head. His heart broke for the kid. Seeing the boy at Pete's funeral, tortured with the pain of losing his dad, had torn Matt apart.

He wiped his hands over his face and closed his eyes.

Forgive me, Lord, for ignoring that call. Let me make it up to Connie and Enrico. Help me find Gallegos.

A string of police cars, lights flashing, blocked St. Ann's. Matt paid the cabby and grabbed his carry-on. Stopped twice by police, he showed his security badge, thankful Wilson had cleared his access.

He double-timed it down the street, glancing up at the wrought iron balconies hanging over the side-walks. Lush pots of jasmine and lilac spilled over the railings, their heady scent in sharp contrast to the rotten stench of garbage waiting for curbside pickup below.

The quiet of the barricaded street seemed out of place in the usually bustling French Quarter. No panhandlers tap-dancing for money, no scurry of pedestrians sipping Hurricanes from tall frosty glasses. Just the eerie quiet of the crime scene.

Don Wilson stood by a patrol car. Tall, late thirties, he turned as Matt approached.

A pinprick of anxiety played over the base of Matt's neck.

Don shook his head as he reached for Matt's outstretched hand. "Bad news."

Matt didn't want excuses.

"We had him surrounded. He was ready to surrender."

"And—"

"Someone got to him before we could. Two shots. Santiago's dead."

TWELVE

The following afternoon, Matt was back at his desk, sipping coffee and staring at his phone. Pulling in a deep breath, he picked up the receiver and dialed. Connie Rodriquez answered on the third ring.

"It's Matt. Just checking up on my favorite little guy."

Connie laughed. "He's sound asleep. Two of his buddies spent the night. Disney DVDs and junk food all night long."

"Bet Mama didn't sleep, either."

"How'd you guess?"

"Connie…" Matt paused, his voice serious. "I got a call from Don Wilson yesterday. They spotted Santiago in New Orleans."

"Matt—"

"He could have led us to Gallegos." Anger and frustration welled up inside him. They had been so close. "Someone made sure he wouldn't talk."

Connie pulled in a sharp breath. "You've got to get past Pete's death."

"When his killer's captured. Even Christ preached justice."

"Justice, not vengeance. Let it go, Matt."

"I can't." He wiped his free hand over his face. "Still praying for me?"

"Every day."

"Keep it up."

An hour later, Matt pulled in behind Lydia's SUV. Stalled on what had happened in New Orleans, he needed to get his mind on something other than Santiago's death.

Tyler sat on the front steps, wearing the fluorescent green goggles.

Matt opened the door to his truck and stepped onto the driveway. "Hey there, buddy."

Tyler jerked his head up. "Chief!"

"Looks like you're ready for the water."

Tyler nodded his head. The goggles magnified his eyes. Matt stifled a laugh at his comical appearance.

"I was waiting for you."

The boy's honesty touched Matt.

Lydia stepped onto the porch and waved. "Hey, Matt. I was in the kitchen. Didn't hear you drive up."

"Just arrived."

She glanced down at Tyler. "You can't read with those goggles on, young man. How are you going to finish that library book?"

Tyler's shoulder's slouched forward. The kid tried to look dejected. Matt winked at Lydia.

Suddenly Tyler's face broke into a wide grin. "Can we go swimming today?"

Matt smiled. "Better ask your mom first."

"Can I, Mom?"

"Sure you don't have more important things to do?" she asked Matt.

"I said I'd teach him. Might as well get started."

Tyler jumped to his feet. "I'll put on my suit." The boy raced past Lydia and into the house before she could stop him.

She laughed. "He's been driving me crazy to go swimming. Not that I blame him."

"I can teach two just as easy as one."

"No, thanks. I'll sit on the shore." She looked at her watch. "When do you want to meet at the beach?"

Matt remembered the way she had raced out of the picnic park after the sand castle contest. He didn't want her running scared today.

"I've got my suit in the truck. We can drive there together."

Lydia thought for a moment, then nodded. "Go ahead and change in the spare bathroom."

After Matt slipped into his bathing trunks and T-shirt, he walked back outside, threw his uniform behind the seat of his pickup and pulled out a plastic bag.

Handing it to Tyler, Matt said, "Thought you might like something special for the beach now that you're learning to swim."

The boy pulled a bright red towel from the bag. "Cool! It's got the A.P. logo on it. Where'd you get it?"

"Ran into a friend of mine when I was out of town. He collects all kinds of A.P. stuff."

"Look what the chief gave me," Tyler said as Lydia stepped outside in a swimsuit and coverup that matched her blue eyes.

"Did you say, 'Thank you'?"

Tyler gave Matt a hug. "Thanks, Chief. It's awesome."

Clutching the beach towel, Tyler climbed into the truck, and Lydia slid in next to him with her tote bag. Teaching the boy to swim would get Matt's mind off Gallegos. Of course, it wouldn't keep his thoughts off Lydia.

The way she looked, he doubted he could keep his mind on anything else.

As soon as they arrived at the community beach, Tyler spread out his towel, then ran to the water's edge and slipped on the goggles. He padded along the shoreline, leaving footprints in the soggy sand.

Lydia watched her son. Since the incident on the playground, she had yearned to see him happy again. Maybe their lives were returning to normal, after all.

The fresh air invigorated her. She and Tyler had spent the morning holed up in the stuffy library. Thankfully, the head librarian was nowhere in sight. Lydia didn't need raised eyebrows or grunts of disapproval from someone who had no idea why she was searching the Web.

If only Katherine had a computer. Unfortunately, she claimed cyberspace was beyond her grasp. Her home was filled with the latest technology, just not a P.C.

Matt pulled off his shirt and all thoughts of computers vanished. The guy must lift weights by the looks of his muscles.

"Race you to the water," he called to Tyler and laughed as the boy ran into the waves. Matt was right behind him and scooped him into his arms, then twirled him around as the water broke around their legs.

Tyler screamed with delight and yelled at Lydia as she laid a second towel on the beach. "Hey, Mom. Look at us."

She laughed and waved back.

Matt lowered Tyler into the water, continuing to hold on to him. There wasn't an ounce of fear on his little face. He stretched out his body and kicked his feet. Matt turned him onto his back, and before long, Tyler was floating on his own.

Each time he accomplished a task, he yelled, "Mom, did you see me?"

"Good for you, honey. You're swimming," she called back.

The sun was bright, but a breeze kept the afternoon from getting too hot. Lydia walked to the water's edge and cooled her feet in the low surf, waving when Tyler looked at her for approval.

Matt proved to be a good teacher. After about an hour, Tyler had enough confidence to do a simple backstroke without help.

"He'll be doing the Australian crawl in no time," Matt called to Lydia, then ruffled Tyler's wet hair. "That's enough for today, buddy. You need to give your muscles a rest. Stay at the water's edge and play for a while. Your mom and I will watch you from the shore."

Tyler splashed in the shallow water, chased the waves and seagulls and made motorboat sounds while Lydia and Matt sat on the beach.

Lydia sighed deeply. "I feel more relaxed than I have in months."

"It's the ocean. Problems drift away with the tide."

"I never liked the beach." She glanced at the sandpipers scurrying along the water's edge foraging for food. Had there been sandpipers that day? All she remembered was her dad's stern command to swim.

The memory flooded over her. She had gasped for air, struggling to keep her head above water, while her mother stood by silently watching, fear of her husband holding her back.

Matt touched Lydia's arm. "You okay?"

She turned to face him, pulled in a deep breath and slowly exhaled. Fast-forward twenty-three years. Matt sat next to her, not her dad.

She nodded. "Yeah, I'm fine."

"A lot of people fear water."

"I'm not afraid."

He raised an eyebrow.

"Okay. So maybe a little," she admitted.

"Face your fear, and you'll start to control it. I can teach you."

"Another day."

He glanced away, studied the horizon, then turned back to her. "Not too many days left. I'm leaving Sanctuary in a couple weeks."

Lydia's eyes widened. "What?"

"As soon as the Island Association finds a new security chief."

"But Tyler's swimming lessons?" Lydia felt her stomach turn over.

"Two weeks and he'll be a pro."

Tyler idolized Matt even just in the short time they'd become acquainted. Now someone else her son cared about would walk out of his life.

"I suppose you're going back to law enforcement?" she said, disappointment evident in her voice.

"Matter of fact, my old job's available."

"Miami, huh?"

"I'm not sure where I'll end up. Maybe Miami. Or New Orleans." He glanced at her. "Maybe even Atlanta."

A chill swept over her, and she shivered despite the heat of the day.

If Matt talked to the cops in Atlanta, he'd learn the police thought she had started the fire.

Something she didn't want him to know.

She turned to Tyler, playing in the sand. "Rinse off, honey. It's time to go home."

The idyllic surroundings of island life had lulled her into a false sense of security. The fire and all that had happened in Atlanta seemed a lifetime ago. But nothing had changed.

The police still believed she was to blame for her husband's death, and until she could uncover evidence to the contrary, she and Tyler wouldn't be safe...not here on Sanctuary Island.

Not anywhere.

THIRTEEN

Tyler's chatter filled the pickup as they drove back from the beach. Lydia didn't say a word.

Matt was sure she had enjoyed the afternoon. Laughing and waving at her son as he floated in the water, she looked happier than Matt had ever seen her. Until he had mentioned Atlanta.

Then her mood changed fast as lightning.

He was still thinking about Lydia's reaction when he stepped into his office and heard the phone ring.

"Security. Lawson."

"Matt, it's Luke Davenport. Afraid I don't have good news about the search for a new security chief. Hard to find anyone interested in a small island community. The Association wondered if that new hire of yours, Butch Griffin, might be able to fill the bill. At least on a temporary basis."

Matt lowered himself into his chair. "I'm not sure, Luke. The guy hasn't been here long."

"You're right. We're rushing the point. But we

know you want to move on. Think about it, Matt. In the meantime, we'll keep looking."

Matt hung up and wiped his hand over his chin. Horwitz wouldn't hold his old job open for much longer. Matt needed to make a decision about Butch, and soon.

The phone rang again.

"You've hired yourself quite a cop in that Butch Griffin," the mainland sheriff said as soon as Matt answered the call. "I told you about the guy who liked his liquor and admitted peeking into windows over on the island?"

"Said you locked him up on drug charges," Matt replied.

"That's right. But once the alcohol dried up and the drugs cleared out of his system, he denied the Peeping Tom charge. Said he'd been framed. That's when Griffin stepped in again."

"How so, Wayne?"

"He found our mainland burglar."

"You mean, the Peeping Tom confessed?"

"Affirmative. Griffin tells him we'll go easy on him if he talks. All of a sudden, he's singing like a canary."

"So everything's wrapped up nice and pretty," Matt said.

"Outstanding police work, in my opinion. I'd say Griffin needs a raise."

"He just started working."

"Yeah. Well, you keep him around, hear me? He's

an asset. Might think about having him step into your shoes when you leave."

"You been talking to Luke Davenport?"

"No, why?"

"Just a hunch," Matt said before he hung up.

Butch Griffin had tied up the mainland break-in case in short order.

Wayne Turner had nothing but praise for the new hire, but it was too easy.

'Course, Matt wasn't a good judge of anything right about now. His earlier discussion with Lydia had put a bad spin on the day. She had a powerful effect on him…and not all positive.

Face your fear, he had told her. Might as well follow his own advice.

He picked up the phone and dialed the library. "Muriel, this is Chief Lawson."

He hated to broach the subject, but he needed to tie up loose ends before he left the island. "Have you seen that woman around the library anymore? The one who logged on the porn Web site?"

"Not me. But Juanita worked this morning and said she was back. Spent an hour or so staring at the computer. Even printed off a few pages. Thank goodness her son stays in the children's section. Wouldn't want a little guy to see the likes of what's on that screen."

"You happen to know the URL?"

"Yes, I checked the computers that first day after she left. Juanita did the same today. I've trained her to keep an eye out for *those* types. The more we can learn about what they're doing, the better."

Matt didn't want to hear any more of Muriel's nonsense.

"Mind telling me the site?"

She gave him the URL.

Matt hung up and booted up his computer, went online and typed in the site.

The home page flashed before him.

What he saw made him want to jam his fist into the monitor.

"Head for the bathtub, young man," Lydia ordered Tyler when they came home from the beach. "Wash off all that sand and salt while I fix dinner."

Tyler's eyes were heavy when he dragged himself to the table. Lydia smiled. Her son's first day in the water had left him tired but happy. Thanks to Matt.

And she'd overreacted. Just because Matt was thinking of working in Atlanta didn't mean he'd exchange information with the cops who had given her a hard time. Once again, she had let her own fear get in the way of common sense.

She'd apologize tomorrow.

Children were resilient. Tyler would get over Matt leaving, probably before she would. Part of the problem was she didn't want to say goodbye.

After dinner, she tucked Tyler into bed, then stepped into the master bedroom and locked the door behind her. She didn't want her son walking in and seeing what she had printed off the library computer.

If only Sonny's computer expertise hadn't forced her to study something that went against every fiber in her body. But she was sure Sonny had hidden information on the Men's Club Web site. If history proved anything, it would prove her right.

Just as she'd told the reporter, Sonny had lost a good job with a legitimate computer firm because he manipulated their Web site and added a ribald expression in the background of a photo of the company's headquarters. Merely a joke, he claimed when the CEO called him into his office.

The boss hadn't appreciated Sonny's warped humor.

She laid a copy of the Men's Club home page on the bed, along with shots of the club's interior and the hostesses at work. If Sonny had information to hide, the Web site was a likely place.

The photos of the women turned her stomach. Some were scantily clad and provocatively poised to accentuate their bodies. How could her husband get involved in such filth? She wanted to rip the photos to shreds and flush them down the toilet.

Lydia shook her head. Why did women allow themselves to be exploited? For money? Did they have children to raise and no other way to make a living?

Lydia had cleaned houses when she and Sonny were first married and needed to pay the bills. Not a glamorous job, but honest work.

Ruby supported her mother and handicapped

sister on her paycheck. Her earnings provided the medical treatment Charise needed.

At least Ruby was getting out. Determined to start fresh. She told Lydia, she had made her peace with God. That's what Lydia wanted—a new start. The God part was negotiable.

First, she had to find the evidence her husband had gathered. Sonny told her he was working for an entertainment company, representing a number of restaurant chains in the Southeast. She never saw the site, never questioned his work.

The money was good—too good. That should have been a warning.

After his death, she learned the club had ties with drugs and pornography, even money laundering and gambling. Ruby explained about the back rooms and secret hideaways where anything could be bought for a price. Sonny had seen it all, including the influential people who regularly used the club's special services.

And it had gotten him killed.

Lydia picked up the phone and dialed Ruby's number. Her shift started at 9:00 p.m. More than likely, she'd still be home this early in the evening.

"Yeah?" Ruby answered on the second ring.

"Can you talk?"

"Let me close the bedroom door." Ruby returned a few seconds later. "You took your sweet time to call back."

"Guess I was trying to ignore a bad situation," Lydia said.

"I hear ya. Same as me. Spent too much of my life hopin' things would get better. Finally, realized I had to be the one to make a change."

"Did you see the files?"

"That doorman I told you about looked the other way while I did the search. Everything's been wiped clean."

Lydia's shoulders slumped.

"But guess who I saw in one of the back rooms 'bout a week ago?"

Before Lydia could answer, Ruby continued, "One of Atlanta's finest."

"Police?"

"You got that right. He's takin' full advantage of the Velvet Room. Reserved for the top dogs. All specialty jobs with the blond, blue-eyed beauties. Usually reserved for the high rollers. Only this time it's a guy from Vice."

"You recognized him?"

"A girlfriend did. He was a thorn in her side years ago when she was turnin' tricks down on Stewart Avenue. Said he's got a mean streak a mile long. According to her, he left Atlanta a few years ago. Moved south. Only now he's back, wearing a five-hundred-dollar suit and getting the full Monty, if you know what I mean."

Lydia thought of the A.P. digital the man in the photo had worn. "Did you happen to notice if he was wearing a watch?"

"A gold Rolex worth more that I'll make in a lifetime."

"Did he see you, Ruby?"

"Not that I know of. Still I'm clearin' out. Mama and Charise think we're gonna visit relatives. Only we're not stoppin' until we're far, far away."

"Be careful."

"Don't worry about us. We'll make it. Just be sure you don't end up like Sonny. You and that boy of yours. Stay away from Atlanta. Leastways till all this blows over. You don't want to be messin' with this cop. From what my friend said, he's one bad dude."

"What's his name?" Lydia asked.

"Hmm? Let me think. Something like Saharis, Polaris," Ruby said. "I don't remember exactly. Maybe Farris."

FOURTEEN

"Time for a break," Matt said to Tyler the next day at the beach. The two of them had been hard at work on the Australian crawl. "Get a drink and take a rest on shore."

"Hey, Mom." Tyler waved to Lydia as he lumbered toward the blanket where she sat. "Chief says I need a break."

She held out a juice box and a bag of trail mix. "Here's a snack."

He sank to the blanket, wiped his face on his A.P. towel, then reached for the juice and dried fruit and smiled with appreciation.

Lydia rose and walked to the water's edge where Matt stood. She raised her hand to her forehead, shielding her eyes from the sun.

"I'm sorry about yesterday, Matt."

"You apologized when I picked you up today, Lydia."

"It's just that Tyler's had so much loss in his life. You mean a lot to him. I don't want him to be hurt again."

Matt's voice was sincere. "That's the last thing I'd want. You had every right to be upset. But I promise, I'll teach Tyler to swim before I leave."

"He loves the water."

"Maybe something his mother should try?" Matt held out his hand. "Let's give it a whirl."

She looked into Matt's eyes. He was leaving in two weeks, but this was today. No reason to worry about tomorrow.

Placing her hand in his, Lydia stepped into the water. The waves washed around her, and she giggled with exhilaration. With Matt at her side, she felt safe and secure.

Cupping his hand around his mouth, Matt shouted to shore. "Tyler, watch your mom. She'll be floating in no time."

Her son gave her a thumbs-up.

"Male conspiracy," she groaned, sending Matt a frosty glare. "Don't let me go under."

"Yes, ma'am."

Reaching for her shoulders, he gently nudged her into the water, supporting her with his hands.

She looked up and saw the blue sky and the fluffy clouds and Matt's handsome face smiling down at her, his eyes encouraging.

Her arms billowed out to her sides, buoyed by the saltwater. The natural movement of the ocean lulled her into a peaceful rhythm.

She was weightless, totally relaxed.

Matt's fingers rubbed across her back, then—

"Matt!"

He let go.

She jerked forward, tried to right herself and went under. The water swirled around her. She struggled to find her footing, sank deeper, her arms flailing.

Matt grabbed her shoulders and pulled her up.

Salt burned her eyes and throat. Streams of water ran down her cheeks. Her wet hair lay plastered around her face.

"I didn't…" She coughed. "I didn't want to go under."

"You were floating, Lydia."

"But—"

"Shush. No buts. You were floating by yourself, pure and simple."

She looked at the water, then the shore where Tyler played in the sand and back at Matt's face filled with pride at her accomplishment. Pushing her hair back, she pouted for a moment.

"My face got wet."

"Lydia—"

Before he could finish the statement, the waves forced them together.

"I'm proud of you," he said.

A warm glow wrapped around her.

Matt stepped even closer. "Lydia, I—"

"Mom!" Tyler called from shore.

She pulled her gaze from Matt.

"Way to go, Mom!"

Matt let out a deep breath and stepped back. "Guess that wraps it up for today."

For the first time in her life, Lydia didn't want to get out of the water, but as Matt stepped toward shore, she followed. Both of them walked in silence until the sound of an approaching car caused them to turn.

"What the—" Matt groused.

Black car, tinted windows.

Lydia ran to Tyler and pulled him into her arms.

"What's wrong?" He tried to wiggle out of her embrace.

"Hey!" Matt yelled at the driver.

The car braked to a stop and the door swung open.

"The association passed an ordinance against driving on the beach," Matt said between clinched teeth.

Joel stepped onto the sand, his eyes flashed in defiance. "Don't give me that, Lawson. Security vehicles always patrol this area."

"Police and security have access. Private vehicles aren't allowed."

Joel shrugged. "Guess I'm ignorant of the rules."

"Ignorant, all right. Next time, it's a five-hundred-dollar fine."

"Like I care. I've *tipped* people that much," Joel replied.

Matt lowered his voice and stepped closer. "I can raise the amount, if you like."

Joel's eyes narrowed, but he climbed into his car and waved to Lydia before he closed the door.

She didn't respond. Her heart was lodged in her throat. She couldn't get past the memory of the school yard in Atlanta.

Releasing her hold on Tyler, she said, "Pick up your things, honey. We're going home."

"Mr. Cowan's not the bad guy, Mom."

"You never know," Matt said, watching Joel's car disappear from sight. "Some people aren't who they seem."

FIFTEEN

The swimming lessons continued over the next few days. Tyler took to the water as if he'd been swimming his whole life. Lydia progressed more slowly.

She knew time was running out. Matt was leaving Sanctuary and Katherine would soon return home from Ireland.

Lydia needed access to a better computer than the models at the library. Plus, the stuffy librarian's body language made it clear Lydia had worn out her welcome. Which left her no choice but to turn to Matt for help.

Lydia dropped Tyler at the Jackson's home and then steered her SUV along Cove Road. Matt was tied up at the courthouse with the arraignment of the man arrested for the mainland break-ins. When Lydia asked if she could use Matt's computer to contact old friends in Atlanta, he had gladly agreed and had given her a key.

She turned into the parking lot, grateful no other cars were in sight and checked her watch: one-thirty.

Bobby's dad was taking the boys to the movies on the mainland. Tyler would be gone for almost three hours. Hopefully, enough time to find clues Sonny might have left on the Web site.

Stepping into Matt's office, Lydia spied the photo of the small boy. Intrigued, she removed the frame from the wall and turned it over.

To Matt, from your favorite catcher, the inscription read. Enrico Rodriquez was scribbled in a childish script.

Matt's partner's son. Lydia could imagine the guilt Matt carried. He blamed himself for his partner's death and for a little boy losing his father.

Tyler had struggled with the pain and confusion surrounding Sonny's death. Seeing her son's grief had torn her apart. Maybe she and Matt shared that in common.

She returned the photo.

As she moved to the desk, her finger trailed over the bookcase where criminal justice texts filled the shelves. His Bible sat on the edge of his desk. She touched the worn leather briefly before she slipped into Matt's desk chair, tapped Enter to delete the screen saver and double clicked on Internet Explorer. Keying in the Men's Club URL, she hit Search and waited for the home page to appear.

The club's logo twirled in the top right-hand corner. A menu scrolled across the bottom. Lydia clicked on the virtual tour and waited as the photos unrolled. A pouting redhead led the parade, followed by a plus-sized blonde and an Asian-American with cocoa skin and almond eyes.

The women's suggestive poses sickened Lydia. She looked away. She'd seen enough to last a lifetime.

Despite the unpleasant subject matter, she had to study the frames for clues and forced her eyes back to the monitor.

Lydia's senses hardened to the scenes appearing one after another. Intent on finding clues, she didn't have time to be angry or offended. For all his faults, Sonny was a genius when it came to computers. If he had hidden evidence on the Web site, Lydia needed to find it.

After filtering through a dozen series of photos, she glanced at the clock: three-fifteen.

"New" flashed in bold fluorescent neon. She double clicked.

"How's it going?" Matt's voice startled her.

Lydia looked up to see him standing in the doorway, the computer screen hidden from his view. She pushed the escape button as he stepped into the room.

Her heart caught in her throat. She tried to smile but her face froze.

He rounded the desk just as the Web site closed.

Lydia's cheeks burned, her throat dry as the Mojave Desert. "Finished," she managed to mumble, rising from the chair. "How was the court hearing?"

"The judge ruled there was enough evidence for a trial." He glanced down at the monitor. "E-mail work okay?"

"Perfect. Thanks for letting me use your computer. In fact, why don't you come over for dinner tonight? That's the least I can do after you've been so kind."

"Sounds great."

The office door opened, and a tall young man stepped inside.

"Lydia, I don't think you've met Jason Everett, a member of the security team."

Jason stuck out his right hand. "Pleased to meet you, ma'am."

She returned the handshake.

The door opened again. This time a young woman, early twenties and very pregnant, stepped inside.

"Natalie? What are you doing here?" Jason asked, seemingly flustered.

The girl had big eyes and a sweet smile, and from the look on her face, she wished she had something to do with her hands instead of wrapping them around her protruding midriff.

"Looking for my dad. He said he'd come back to the office after that court case. I was in the neighborhood and thought I'd drop by."

She glanced around the room. "Has he been here?"

"The mainland sheriff wanted to see him." Matt stretched out his hand. "I'm Chief Lawson. We met some time ago."

She returned the handshake. "I remember. When Jason and I were going out."

Lydia picked up on the past tense. So the mother-to-be and Jason were no longer an item.

"And this is Lydia Sloan. She's new to Sanctuary."

"Nice to meet you," Natalie said.

Lydia noticed her bare left hand.

"When's your baby due?" Small talk might help to calm the girl's nervousness.

"Another month."

"Have you decided on any names?"

"The doctor thinks it's a boy, but the sonogram was kind of fuzzy. I planned on calling him William after my stepdad, but…" She hung her head for a minute and studied the floor.

"Now that my real dad's back in my life, I'm thinking about Eddie. Edward's his name. 'Course everyone always calls him Butch."

"You and your dad doing okay?" Jason asked, concern evident in his voice.

The girl nodded. "Kind of awkward at first. You know what I mean?" She glanced at Lydia who smiled to encourage her.

"Dad and I hadn't seen each other in years. I wouldn't say things are good, but they're getting better." She looked back at Jason. "He likes working with you."

The kid shoved his hands in his pockets. "We've teamed up on a few patrols."

"Guess I shouldn't have said the things I did about him when we were in high school."

"It's okay."

"Tough not having a dad," Natalie said.

Was she speaking for herself or her unborn child? Either way, the girl's situation touched Lydia.

"I better head back to the mainland," Natalie said. "Tell Butch I stopped by."

"I'll walk you to your car." Jason held the door and followed her outside.

"I'm afraid Jason's still carrying a torch for that little honey," Matt said after they left the room.

"My guess is she feels the same about him."

Matt raised an eyebrow. "You think so?"

"Pretty evident from what I saw. So who's the baby's father?"

"Some guy who skipped town."

"Not Jason?"

"If Jason *is* the father, he doesn't have a clue," Matt said.

Lydia sighed. "And people say there's nothing like young love."

"Makes me glad I'm older."

The look Matt gave her made Lydia catch her breath. She pulled her eyes away and glanced at her watch. "Tyler'll be home soon. Give me an hour to get dinner ready."

She glanced over her shoulder and waved goodbye.

Matt had a point about young love. Look where it had gotten her—married to Sonny, who left her running from a faceless threat.

Maybe Matt leaving Sanctuary would be good for both of them. She couldn't change the fact that she was beginning to care about a man who watched over her and Tyler, taught them to swim and turned her insides to jelly. If he stayed, he might end up in danger just by knowing her.

One thing for sure, she didn't want anything to happen to Matt.

SIXTEEN

After sending Tyler outside to burn off some energy, Lydia worked quickly and soon had everything ready for Matt's arrival. With twenty minutes to spare, she raced into Katherine's bedroom, stroked blush over her cheeks and applied a fresh coat of lipstick.

She was wearing the same sundress she'd worn to Matt's office. The crisp cotton held its shape, and she didn't have time to iron anything else. Besides, Matt was coming for dinner and a relaxing evening. No reason to read any more into her invitation or his acceptance. Still, it felt good to primp a little. She spritzed a floral body spray along her arms and winked at the reflection staring approvingly back at her from the mirror.

On her way to the kitchen, Lydia noticed the sliding-glass door partially open. Tyler must have forgotten to pull it closed.

She stuck her head outside and called, "Come in and wash your hands and face, honey. Chief Lawson will be here in a few minutes."

She looked around the backyard.

"Tyler?"

Stepping onto the deck, her eyes roamed the wooded area that edged the house.

"Where are you, Tyler?"

He knew his boundaries—the deck and yard. No farther. A thread of fear raced along her veins. Where was her son?

The sound of the surf, crashing on the shore, exploded around her.

The beach?

Tyler wouldn't have strayed that far. The shoreline was strictly off-limits.

Lydia ran to the edge of the lawn and searched the beach that lay beyond.

"Tyler," she called again.

And then she saw him. A small speck of blond hair and red shirt.

Her heart stopped beating.

He was in the water, caught in the current, heading toward the open sea.

Lydia slipped down the path to the beach, righted herself, then raced along the sand. *Faster*. She had to get to her son.

"I'm coming," she screamed.

Angry waves pounded against the shore. Dark green water swirled like a vengeful monster. White foam sprayed in the air and danced on the wind.

She ran into the churning sea. Water soaked her dress, weighed her down as if a thousand hands were yanking her back to shore.

The tiny red spot bobbed in the distance. She struggled to move forward.

A wave crashed over her. She gasped, swallowed water. Her nose and throat burned. Salt stung her eyes. She wiped her hand over her face.

Where was Tyler? Squinting toward the horizon, she searched for some sign of him.

The smudge of red reappeared in the distance. Tiny arms flailed in the air. Her heart wrenched in two. She had to save her son.

Stubbing her foot on a submerged rock, she almost fell, caught herself and continued on.

A little farther and she'd be in over her head. Nothing mattered except reaching Tyler.

Another wave washed over her. Her eyes burned, the back of her nose on fire as she snorted the caustic brine.

She opened her mouth to take in a breath and dropped into a deep abyss as the sandbar disappeared beneath her feet. She came up coughing and gasping for air.

The red speck disappeared in the distance. She gulped another mouthful and went under. Clawing the water, she tried to reach the surface.

Something brushed against her leg.

Shark?

She kicked, furiously trying to escape the predator.

Suddenly, she was being propelled upward.

She struggled against the force.

"No!" she screamed as her head broke the surface.

Wiping the water from her eyes, she jerked around. Matt had hold of her, his face close to hers, his arm supporting her.

"Tyler," she managed to gasp.

"I see him. Float, Lydia," Matt ordered. "The rip current's passed. The waves will take you in."

He shoved her toward shore. "Ten feet and you'll be able to touch bottom. You've got to make it. For Tyler's sake."

For Tyler, Lydia thought.

Oh, God, save my son.

Trust me. The words returned in a flash.

She relaxed her muscles and allowed the waves to carry her.

Then she thought of Tyler so far from shore. Would Matt get to him in time?

Her body tensed. She started to go under.

Matt didn't want to turn Lydia loose. He had taught her how to stay afloat and do a simple crawl, but she still feared putting her head in the water. Relying on her own version of the dog paddle, she'd make it to the sandbar, where she could touch ground. If she didn't panic.

Out of the corner of his eye, he watched her struggle toward shore. A few feet more and she'd be out of danger.

Tyler was another story. As the waves dipped, Matt saw the spot of red in the middle of the dark, choppy sea.

"Hold on, Tyler," he said. "Hold on, son."

If the boy would do a dead man's float and not struggle against the current, he might be able to conserve his energy and survive until Matt reached him.

Let him remember what I taught him, Lord. And thank You for getting me here just in time.

Matt prided himself on being punctual. Arriving ahead of schedule wasn't his style. Yet an urgency to get to Lydia's had picked at him like a fly hovering over a picnic lunch until he climbed into his pickup and headed up Cove Road. Fifteen minutes early.

Now he knew why.

When no one had answered the door, he had circled the house to the deck, hoping to find Lydia and Tyler. It hadn't taken long for him to realize something was wrong.

Seeing Lydia flailing in the water and Tyler far out at sea, Matt raced to the water's edge, kicked out of his shoes and ripped off his shirt.

He had to save Tyler. If something happened to the boy, Matt wouldn't be able to live with himself. The pain would be too great.

God, help me.

A strong stroke propelled Matt forward. Right arm. Left arm. Right arm. He kept his head up and his eyes on the boy.

The distance narrowed. Tyler's head bobbed in the water.

Closer, closer.

A large wave loomed ahead.

"Hold on, Tyler," Matt screamed as the water crashed over the child.

Frantically, Matt swam to the spot where the red shirt had been.

He dived below the surface.

Where was the boy?

Matt had to find him.

Seconds passed too quickly.

He swam deeper, searching, his eyes burning from the salt, his lungs ready to tear in two.

There. Tyler!

Matt grabbed the child's shirt. He wrapped an arm around the small torso and pulled the limp body into his arms.

With powerful kicks, Matt broke the surface and turned the boy over.

"Tyler. Wake up, Tyler. I've got you. You're going to be okay."

Matt held the boy in his arms as he treaded water, willing life back into the small body.

"Tyler, open your eyes."

Dear God, don't let this child die.

The boy gasped for air. His eyes fluttered open. Fear flashed across his face. He coughed and pulled in a ragged breath.

"You're okay, son," Matt said. "I've got you now."

"I...I did what you said, Chief. I floated like a jellyfish."

Matt wanted to laugh with relief, but they were far

from shore and still in danger. He had to get Tyler back to Lydia.

"I'm going to wrap my arm around you, Tyler. Lie back against me. I'll paddle us to shore."

The boy did as Matt asked. Slipping his arm over Tyler's chest, Matt tucked him against his left hip. There the boy could ride out the waves while Matt stroked the water with his free hand. Just so they wouldn't be caught in another rip current.

"Good job, Tyler. Relax. Let me do the work."

He could feel the rapid beat of the boy's heart.

"That's it, son. You're doing fine."

When they made it to the sandbar, Matt dropped his feet and looked at shore. Where was Lydia?

He wanted to shout her name and crash through the waves, searching for her. He had saved her son, but—

Then he saw her, running through the water toward them.

"Tyler!" she screamed. "Are you all right?"

Matt pulled the boy out of the water. "Tell your mom you're fine."

"Mom," the boy cried out. "Matt saved me."

Tears streamed down Lydia's face. She ran to them, pulled Tyler into her arms and clutched him to her heart.

"Let's get to dry land." Matt urged them through the shallow water. On shore, he grabbed his shirt and shoes and tried to take Tyler from Lydia. She wouldn't turn him loose.

With tears of gratitude running down her cheeks,

she carried Tyler to the deck, then sat on a chair and wrapped him ever more tightly in her arms.

"Mom!" the boy finally complained.

"Oh, Tyler, I thought I'd lost you. The water…"

She looked up at Matt. He shook his head to warn her. Tyler had been through enough. She didn't need to add her own fears to the boy's.

An understanding passed between them. She nodded almost imperceptibly. "Honey, you know the ocean's off-limits in this area."

Tyler ducked his head.

She placed her finger on his chin. "Look at me. Why did you break the rules and go into the water?"

"I was playing on the beach," the boy mumbled.

"And?"

"My Frisbee, Mom." His eyes clouded, and it looked as if he might burst into tears. "It went in the water."

"And you ran after it?"

He hung his head and nodded.

Lydia hugged him close. Ironic. She'd brought Tyler to the remote island to get away from the Atlanta threat and keep him safe.

Maybe coming here had been a mistake.

She looked up at the man who had saved her son.

Then again, she *had* found something worthwhile in Sanctuary.

SEVENTEEN

Lydia couldn't take her eyes off Tyler as Matt carried the boy inside the house. She gave him a hot bath and dressed him in warm pajamas before she slipped into something dry. When she came back into the kitchen, Matt had changed into the spare clothes he kept in his truck.

While Tyler played with Legos on the living room floor, Lydia finished the meal preparation, peering in at him every few minutes. As much as she didn't feel like eating, keeping a sense of normalcy would be good for all of them.

Matt grilled a steak. She tossed the salad and removed the potatoes from the oven. When they sat at the kitchen table, she looked at her son and was filled with gratitude.

"Trust me," a voice had whispered to Lydia when Tyler was being carried out to sea. Could the Lord have spoken to her heart? Had He sent Matt at the exact moment to save her son? Or was it coincidence that Matt had arrived in the nick of time?

She wasn't ready to give God full credit. She needed more proof before her seed of faith grew larger. Still, she owed Him a word of thanks. But finding her voice with the Almighty was beyond her grasp at the moment.

"Matt, would you give thanks before we eat?"

The three of them joined hands and bowed their heads.

"Dear Lord, thank You for the food we are about to eat and for allowing us to be together this evening. We know You are a God who loves us and cares for our every need. Continue to watch over us, Lord, and protect us from harm. Amen."

Matt ate with relish, but Tyler toyed with his food, his eyes heavy. When he could no longer hold his head upright, Lydia scooped him into her arms, her own food ignored.

"Bedtime," she said to Matt.

Carrying her sleepy child into his room, she pulled down the spread and laid the boy on the bed.

He snuggled under the covers. "Sorry my Frisbee went in the water, Mom."

She tousled his hair. "The Frisbee's not important. But you are, Tyler. I love you so very much."

"I know, Mom."

"When I tell you something, there's a reason. Usually, it's to keep you safe."

He swallowed hard.

"If you don't understand, ask me. We can talk about it. Okay?"

"I will. I promise."

She rubbed her hand down his cheek. "And always tell Mama the truth."

His eyes grew wide. "Always, Mom. Cross my heart. But Bobby said he makes up stories sometimes."

"Oh?"

"When his mom and dad fight."

"All parents have disagreements, honey."

"I know, Mom. I told him he has to tell the truth, no matter what." Tyler bit his lip. "Chief says I'm a good swimmer. I would have been okay today, 'cept the waves pulled me out too far."

Lydia leaned over her son and kissed his cheek. "You're safe now, Tyler. Go to sleep, honey."

She watched his eyes shut and his breathing slip into a steady rhythm. She'd almost lost him for the second time. A loving God wouldn't allow such a thing to happen.

Would He?

Matt stood when Lydia entered the living room, and his heart caught in his throat. He'd never seen her look more beautiful. Before dinner, she had pulled her hair back from her face in a ponytail and donned the polka-dot shorts and blouse she'd worn that first afternoon on the beach. But it was the sense of relief and gratitude that he saw written so clearly on her face, that tugged at his heart.

Her eyes met his, and she stopped walking. "I…I don't know how to thank you."

He shrugged. "Seems I got my timing right."

"I can't imagine what might have happened if you hadn't been there."

She shivered, and Matt wanted to take her in his arms and hold her tight. She'd been through a lot, and he sensed the tension that still pounded through her body.

"I tried to save him," she said, her voice not much more than a whisper. "If only I hadn't waited so long to start the swimming lessons. I've been so stubborn." She sighed. "So stupid."

He crossed the room and placed his hands on her shoulders. She looked into his eyes.

"Lydia, you did everything you could. The current was strong. Even if you'd been a better swimmer, it's doubtful you could have pulled him from the rip current. You and Tyler might both have been lost."

Her eyes searched his. "You saved us, Matt."

He shook his head. "God did it, Lydia. He nagged me to get here early. When I saw you flailing in the water, it all became clear."

Her puzzled look made him continue.

"About a year ago, there was talk that the guy who killed my partner was operating in this area. I told myself the security job would give me the chance to find him. In reality, I was hiding out."

She wrinkled her brow. "From what?"

"From my own guilt. I was with a woman the night Pete needed me. I didn't answer my cell, and he went into the raid before backup arrived. It cost him his life."

"Everyone makes mistakes, Matt."

"I put myself first, something partners never do."

She shook her head. "You're too hard on yourself."

"That's what Pete's wife told me." Matt sighed, remembering Connie's disregard of her own grief to help him work through his.

"I asked God's forgiveness," he continued. "Thinking if I caught the killer, I'd find redemption."

He gazed down into Lydia's eyes. "God's forgiveness washed over me today in the water. By saving Tyler, God allowed me to save myself."

Lydia looked at him as if she could see into his heart. He hoped she could see the love of the Lord that had taken hold there. He wanted to share that feeling with Lydia. If only she could trust God.

"Maybe God's love will wash over me someday," she whispered.

Her sincerity touched him, and he realized he was falling for Lydia. Hard.

He pulled her into his embrace and lowered his lips to hers.

Lydia woke the next morning thinking of Matt. She smiled, remembering his kiss and the sense of completeness she felt wrapped in his arms.

Tyler was still asleep so Lydia perked coffee and took a cup out onto the deck where she watched the birds skitter through the trees.

She didn't know when she'd felt so rested and refreshed, or when a morning seemed as sparkling clear. Even the ocean that had been a threatening monster yesterday was calm today.

The realization of the fragility of life and the importance of living each moment in the present swept over her. For so long, she had focused on the past. Now she was ready to live for today.

Matt was a good man, so different from Sonny. She could trust Matt. But he deserved to know what a relationship with her entailed.

Tyler had a late-afternoon playdate with Chase. When Luke Davenport and his wife picked Tyler up, Lydia buckled his seat belt and waved goodbye.

"Have fun," she called as the car pulled out of the drive.

Grabbing her purse and keys, Lydia climbed into her SUV and drove to Matt's office. His pickup was the only vehicle in the parking lot.

She knocked before she entered, then stepped into the cool interior. Would he be surprised to see her? Or was she reading too much into one kiss?

A pleased look washed over Matt's face when he glanced up from his desk and saw her standing in the doorway. He was dressed in running shorts and a damp T-shirt.

"I should have called," she said.

"You would have gotten Eunice. I was on a run."

He rose, rounded his desk and was at her side in five long strides. Without saying more, he wrapped her in his arms and pulled her close.

Lydia's muscles weakened and her pulse quickened. All she could think of was being in Matt's arms, as if nothing in the world was as important at this moment.

Matt stared down into her eyes. His right hand played with her hair.

She smiled, seeing the warmth written on his face. "I owe you so much, Matt. Saving Tyler—"

Matt looked behind her. "Where is he?"

"With the Davenports. They picked him up about fifteen minutes ago. Four o'clock matinee and an early dinner. Part of me didn't want to let him go. I wanted to hold on to him even tighter than I had before."

"I don't blame you after all that's happened."

A glow of appreciation filled her. He hadn't told her she was overreacting or too protective, which is what Sonny would have said. Matt could sense her moods and the deep maternal feelings that guided so much of what she did with Tyler.

"I knew it was time to make some changes," she said. "Just like you, I've been hiding out in Sanctuary. That's why Tyler and I came here in the first place. I want to tell you some things I couldn't tell you before, Matt." She looked into his questioning eyes and found the strength and determination she needed to go on.

Lydia told Matt her marriage had ended long before she'd walked into her husband's office and saw the pornography on his computer. She told Matt about her ultimatum for Sonny to leave the illegal operation, and her husband's need to gather evidence, in case the powers that be tried to nail him for their own wrongdoings.

"A week before his death, Sonny had me up the insurance on our house. He must have known something might happen. But he died before he had everything in place."

"Killed in a fire that destroyed your life, as well as his," Matt added.

"Tyler and I moved into an apartment not far from his school. At first I was too numb and confused to realize what was going on around me. But slowly I started to sense the things that happened weren't a coincidence. I felt a sinister presence watching and waiting, as if the people who Sonny had been involved with were trying to determine if I had anything on them. There were footprints in the backyard after a rain, phone calls in the middle of the night." She told him what had happened on the playground. "Someone wanted to frighten us away."

"Seems they got their wish," Matt said.

Lydia nodded. "We ran away after they tried to grab Tyler. I needed to find a place to hide and let things cool off in Atlanta. I didn't think Katherine would stay in Ireland so long. I wanted her to watch Tyler, while I went back to do some digging on my own."

"Did Sonny have a safe-deposit box or a secret locker where he stashed the information?"

She shook her head. "I think he hid it on the Web site."

Matt raised an eyebrow. "Right under their noses?"

"At least some of the information. The Web was Sonny's style."

Lydia told Matt about the prank Sonny had pulled at his former computer firm. "Once the boss learned Sonny tampered with the Web site, he fired him. Tyler had just started a new private school and we needed money to pay the bills. I told Sonny I'd go back to cleaning houses, but he wouldn't hear of it. He told me he found freelance work. I never suspected it involved anything illegal."

"And that's what you were doing at the library, searching the Web site for clues?"

Lydia felt her cheeks burn. "The librarian must have told you."

"Muriel never liked the Internet. She calls me whenever the teenage boys check out the girlie sites. This time it wasn't a teenage boy."

"I needed access to a computer. That's why I asked to use your e-mail."

"I could have helped you."

Lydia bit her lip. "Sonny said the police and some of the leaders in the state and county governments were involved. He told me not to trust anyone. And that meant you, Matt. You were law enforcement for the island."

He touched her cheek and looked longingly into her eyes. "I'd never do anything to hurt you."

Lydia smiled, relieved to have finally told Matt the truth. It felt good to be free of the burden.

"Let me shower and change out of these sweaty clothes," he said. "Then we'll both get on the Net and see what we can find."

"Mind if I make a phone call first? There's a reporter I want to contact. She called me after Sonny died and offered to help."

"Sure, make the call. And if Jason phones, find out about Natalie. He took her to the doctor today. I'll be out in five minutes." He headed for the shower.

Lydia tapped in the number of the *Atlanta Journal-Constitution*.

"Features," a male voice answered.

"Sorry, I…," Lydia stammered. "I must have dialed the wrong number."

"You callin' Trish about a story?"

Lydia straightened her shoulders. Talking to one reporter was hard enough, she didn't want everyone in the newsroom to know about Sonny and the Men's Club. "If she's busy, I can call back."

The guy sniffed. "Where you been, lady?"

"What?"

"Old news by now. You been outta town?"

The guy's questions bothered her. "Look, I apologize…"

"Good reporter. Top-of-the-line, you know what I mean?"

"Yes, of course. Ms. Delaney's the best in the city."

"No *is* about it, lady. Was. Trish Delaney *was* the best. Guess you didn't hear. She's dead. Hit and run when she was walking her dog. Neighbor saw a black

Mercedes, only no one's come forward. A real tragedy, you know what I mean?"

Lydia wanted to agree, but her voice froze. She dropped the phone to the cradle and gasped, forcing air into her lungs.

Trish Delaney dead? It couldn't be. And a black Mercedes.

Oh, dear God, help us all.

The phone rang. Probably Jason with news about Natalie and the baby. She pulled in a deep breath, swallowed and lifted the receiver to her ear.

"Hello?"

"Yeah, let me speak with Matt," a voice demanded.

Not Jason's voice.

Lydia wiped her free hand over her face. Her body had stalled, and she needed to get it back into gear.

"I'm…I'm sorry. He's unavailable." She tried to sound coherent. "May I take a message?"

"Tell him Harris called. Roger Harris, Atlanta P.D."

Polaris? Farris? Harris? Could the voice on the phone belong to the police officer Ruby had seen at the Men's Club?

A wave of nausea washed over Lydia. The room twirled around her, and for a second, she thought she might black out. She blinked to focus her eyes and her thoughts.

Dropping the phone, she rose from the chair. She needed to get Tyler and run away. Away from the Atlanta police, away from the danger, away from Matt.

"Ready to surf the Web?" Matt stepped into the office.

She turned to face him. "Roger Harris called you from the Atlanta P.D."

"What'd he want?"

Lydia's heart pounded in her chest. "I don't know."

Her hands shook. She pulled them behind her back, hoping to hide her nervousness. "Listen, I'd better go. I promised Tyler I'd have cookies baked by the time he got home."

"Don't run off," Matt pleaded.

She avoided his eyes. She'd made a huge mistake confiding in Matt.

"Lydia?"

She heard him call her name, but she'd already walked through the door and slammed it shut behind her.

EIGHTEEN

Matt waited fifteen minutes for Lydia to drive back to Katherine's house before he picked up the phone and dialed her number.

"What's wrong?" he said as soon as she answered. "Was it the phone call from Harris? The cops in Atlanta don't know you're on the island. I didn't betray you."

"Why should I believe you?" she threw back at him.

"Because I care about you, Lydia."

"Don't lie, Matt. You're leaving Sanctuary, remember?"

From the tone of her voice, he knew there was only one way to change her mind.

"I'll search the Net. See what I can uncover."

"You don't have to help me."

"Yeah, but I want to. Call you in the morning." Before hanging up, he remembered her phone call to Atlanta. "What'd the reporter say?"

Lydia was silent for a long minute. "She…she's dead."

"What?"

"Hit and run. Guess what type of car was spotted that night?"

The hair on the back of his neck tingled. "A black Mercedes?"

"Exactly."

"Lock your doors, Lydia. I'll be over in the morning. Jason's scheduled to pull the night shift. I'll have him patrol your area."

Matt hung up, determined to locate any clues Lydia's husband might have left. Lydia had every right to run scared. Sonny's death hadn't been an accident. Someone had wanted him out of the way.

From what she said, the club served as a front. The girlie shows and pornography were probably just the tip of the payload filled with muck and mire that occurred behind their closed doors.

Matt tapped in the address for the club and waited as the site unfolded. A sassy redhead waved while a cartoon kitten in the lower right hand corner beckoned the viewer to delve further. Matt browsed through the photos.

The beguiling looks of the women teased the viewer. Perhaps that's what Sonny wanted—to tease the owners of the operation by leaving enough information on the site to prove he knew what was going on. Enough information to warn everyone to back off. Insurance, he had told Lydia.

But something went wrong. Either the owners hadn't found the evidence or they'd weighed their options and put their money on killing Sonny and worrying about anything he might have left behind after the fact.

It was like searching for Waldo. Except he didn't know what Waldo looked like. Before long, Matt knew he needed the help of an expert.

Vic Wallace came to mind.

Matt found the computer whiz's Miami number in his Rolodex, dialed and waited until a voice rasped hello.

"Hey, buddy. Thanks again for that beach towel. Little guy I know loves it," Matt said.

"Glad to help out. Good Lord blessed me, that's for sure. Nice to pass it on. What's up?"

"Computer problem. Thought you might be up to the challenge."

"Computer challenge?" Vic chuckled. "You've called the right man. I'm all ears."

Matt gave Vic an attenuated version of the story and what he had done so far. "No telling what Sonny buried. Could be anything."

"I'm on it. I'll let you know when I find something."

Matt hung up with mixed feelings. Would Vic find the evidence Sonny had hid? And would it be enough to incriminate the thugs who were after Lydia and Tyler?

Even with Vic's trained eye on the job, Matt still needed to try to find the clues. Working throughout the long night, he scanned photo after photo.

Nothing.

As the first light of day warmed the sky, he pushed his chair back from his desk and rubbed his neck. Tension had built up over the long night.

He glanced at his watch: 5:00 a.m.

If only he had more experience with computers. Hopefully, Vic would be successful.

The phone rang. Matt raised the receiver to his ear.

The sheriff's voice filled the line. "You ever stop working?"

"Morning, Wayne. What can I do for you?"

"Had a problem last night with that guy arraigned for the mainland break-ins."

Matt let out a sigh. "What happened?"

"Doused himself with gasoline. Must have struck a match. Went up in flames before anyone could contain the fire."

"What? How'd he get the gasoline?"

"That's what I'm trying to find out. Have Butch come see me. I want to go over everything the guy told him. See if we can determine who wanted him dead. We've got a murderer on the loose," the sheriff said. "Tell your people to watch their backs."

Matt hung up, frustrated with the sheriff's news as well as his own unproductive Web search. Turning back to his monitor, a text box flashed on the bottom of his screen.

One new message.

Matt double clicked on the box and read the e-mail.

Matt. Piece of cake.

He opened the JPEG.

Leaning into the monitor, Matt studied the photo. Bingo! Vic had found Waldo.

Lydia was waiting on the front porch when the Davenports dropped Tyler off after the movie and dinner.

"We're back a little earlier than planned," Luke Davenport said. "Heard there's a storm brewing off the coast. No cause for alarm yet, but might be a good idea to start boarding up the windows. As I recall, Katherine's house has shutters that slip onto the window frames."

Lydia remembered seeing them in the garage. "Is the storm headed this way?"

"Doubt we'll have more than some wind and rain. Still, better to be prepared. Call if you need help."

The shutters were lightweight aluminum and easy to install. Lydia covered the windows that faced the ocean and left the sliding-glass door to the deck and front windows for later. She spent the rest of the evening packing their belongings and loading them into their SUV. Tyler's life depended on them being safe. After the phone call from Harris, she felt anything but secure in Sanctuary. She and Tyler would leave in the morning.

Later that night, Lydia wrote a note to Katherine, thanking her for her generous hospitality and promising to call when Lydia and Tyler were settled.

Of course, that was the problem. Lydia didn't know where they would go. Or how she would ever find the men who killed her husband. Trish Delaney had offered hope. Now the reporter was dead. Lydia couldn't involve anyone else. The stakes were too high.

Well after midnight, she walked into the guest room and kissed her sleeping son's forehead.

Tyler moaned as his eyelids fluttered open. "I had a bad dream, Mom."

"What was it about, honey?"

He shrugged. "I can't remember."

Lydia soaked a washcloth in tepid water, then wiped it over his face and hands. "Did you have anything to eat at the movie?"

"A hot dog and popcorn."

"Any candy?"

"Chase shared his Rocket Launch with me."

"That colored sugar that comes in the space ship container?" Lydia asked.

Tyler nodded.

Too much sugar and excitement. Next time, she'd limit Tyler's junk food intake. Lydia patted his shoulder until he drifted back to sleep.

Hoping to get a few hours of rest, she headed for the master bedroom where she tossed and turned until dawn. The first light glowed on the horizon when Lydia rose and made her way to the kitchen to perk coffee. A couple mugs of high-test were what she needed.

As she sipped her second cup, a vehicle pulled into the driveway. Her stomach tightened. She peered through the peephole.

Matt's face came into view, and she opened the door before he had a chance to knock.

"Kind of early for a social call," she said, too tired to be angry.

He filled the doorway, lines of fatigue etched around his eyes. His voice carried a sense of urgency as he held up a computer printout.

"A friend of mine who lives and breathes computers found the information. Names of important people. City council, state government, police. You were right. Sonny buried them on the Web site."

Lydia's heart pounded against her chest. "The evidence?"

"Some of it. A tease, it looks like to me. If anyone came too close, Sonny could tell them about the names. One look and they'd know he had information on people whose careers would be ruined if they were tied in with the club."

Lydia motioned Matt inside. "Is it enough?" she asked, closing the door behind him.

"No." Matt walked into the kitchen and spread the papers on the table. "But it's a start. And it's enough for us to take to the chief of police in Atlanta. Hopefully, he'll start an investigation."

She looked at the Web site printout and wrinkled her brow. "I don't see anything."

Matt pointed to the pale lines. "See that pattern in the background?"

Lydia looked where Matt indicated. The letters appeared faint, but she could make out names, flowing one after another.

"Sonny knew his way around a computer," Matt

continued. "He may have hidden even more information. I'll let the chief in Atlanta turn it over to his tech guys. They'll tear it apart pixel by pixel."

"How can you be sure the chief of police isn't involved?"

"He's fairly new to the city. Worked in Iraq for a number of years, setting up their police force. His credentials are impressive, plus he's been out of the country. I'd say he's clean."

"But will he listen to you?"

"I served under him in the military. He'll remember."

Lydia told Matt about her phone call to Ruby. "Did you see Harris's name?"

"No. Are you sure it was Harris your friend recognized at the club? He's a family man—wife and three kids. There's a guy named Paris though. I wouldn't put it past him."

"Ruby had trouble remembering the name," Lydia admitted.

"See if the Jacksons can keep Tyler and come with me. We'll be back tonight. You can tell the police chief your story. He'll listen to you."

Before she could explain that she didn't want to leave Tyler, he stepped into the kitchen.

"Hey, Chief. I thought I heard you talking." Tyler reached out for Lydia.

She pulled him into her arms. "Another bad dream?"

"No, I'm okay." Tyler laid his head on her shoulder and glanced at Matt.

"Tyler had too much sugar yesterday." Lydia saw

a wave of tenderness wash over Matt's face. "You go to Atlanta, Matt. Tyler and I will stay here."

"He can come with us," Matt insisted.

She shook her head. "I won't take Tyler back to Atlanta until the danger's over."

"I don't like leaving you. The list proves the operation is far-reaching. With names that high up, it's got to be major, perhaps with ties to organized crime."

Lydia's skin crawled.

"What's organized crime?" Tyler mumbled from her shoulder.

"Nothing you have to worry about." She patted his back and looked at Matt. "Take the names to Atlanta. We'll be here when you get back."

He smiled, and she liked the way his smile filled his face.

A slow burn started in the pit of her stomach—and it had nothing to do with the temperature in the room.

Matt pulled a cell phone from his pocket and handed it to her. "A storm's headed our way. Sometimes the phone lines go down. Use this cell to reach me on my car phone. The number's programmed in."

Lydia slipped the cell into her pocket. "Luke warned me about the weather when he brought Tyler home."

"Jason's still on duty. Call him if you have any problems. And turn on your alarm."

"Any word on Natalie?"

"The doctor said the baby could come anytime."

Matt kissed Lydia's cheek, then rumpled Tyler's head. "Take care of yourself, buddy."

Lydia locked the door behind Matt, her fear returning full force once his truck pulled out of the drive.

The information proved one thing for sure. She and Tyler were in far more danger than she had ever imagined. Had she drawn Matt in, as well?

NINETEEN

Sixty miles outside Atlanta, Matt turned the air conditioner to high and adjusted the vent. The manila folder holding the computer printout sat on the seat next to him. Luckily, Vic had found the hidden names.

Matt shook his head. Luck wasn't involved.

"Ask and you shall receive."

He'd asked for God's help, and he'd gotten it.

Thank You, Lord.

If only Lydia would realize the power of prayer. He thought back to the night they'd kissed, the memory bringing a smile to his lips.

"Keep your mind on the road," he said aloud, laughing like a schoolboy in love.

Matt turned on the radio and tuned in an easy listening station. Music filled the truck. A woman's fetching soprano told a tale of love and heartbreak that followed one upon the other. His elation plummeted.

If the situation in Atlanta resolved, Lydia would probably head back to the big city. Where would that leave him? Like the singer said, "Alone and lonely with only a memory to hold in the night."

Matt switched the station.

"And now the weather," the announcer said. "The storm off the Southeastern coast of the United States threatens to come ashore by early evening. Storm trackers place the path between Jacksonville and Savannah. Coastal residents are warned to stay vigilant and tuned to local weather stations."

Matt turned off the radio and picked up his car phone. He punched in Lydia's number. Her voice sounded strained when she answered.

"It's Matt."

"I didn't expect to hear from you so soon."

"The weather report said the storm will hit this evening. If it gathers strength you and Tyler need to evacuate. I'll call Jason and have him give you a hand getting off the island."

"He has enough to handle without babysitting the boss's girlfriend."

Matt liked her choice of words.

"We can get to the mainland on our own," Lydia assured him. "When are you coming back to Sanctuary?"

"As soon as I can. Keep your doors locked, Lydia, and use the silent alarm if there's trouble."

Lydia stood on the deck, studying the darkening sky. A storm had welcomed them to Sanctuary and now another might force them to leave.

So much had happened since their arrival. She had found a man who cared for her, a man Tyler adored. In her heart, she knew Matt wanted what was best for both of them. That's why he was headed to Atlanta to turn in the information Sonny had collected, information that would bring an end to their ordeal.

Rain began to fall, and she raced back into the house. Tyler was in his room, packing a few toys in his backpack.

"I've got my Action-Pac," he said, tapping the zipper compartment of his tote. When he looked up at her, his face was lined with worry.

"What's wrong, honey?"

"Remember when you checked the game discs, Mom?"

Right after the fire. "Yes, I remember."

"I forgot to give one of them to you. It didn't work so I threw it in the trash." He glanced at the can in the corner. "That's okay, isn't it, Mom?"

"Of course."

He hesitated for a long moment, brow wrinkled. "What about Dad's pocketknife?"

Lydia looked down at her child. Sonny had promised Tyler could have the knife when he turned ten. She had found it in the rubble of the fire and tucked it in her handbag for safekeeping.

"The knife's in my purse. I won't forget it."

He nodded, and for a second, Tyler looked years older than his age. He was growing up too fast. Let him be a boy for a little longer.

"Finish packing while I call Bobby's mom," she said, leaving his room. In the kitchen, she picked up the phone and tapped in the Jacksons' number.

"It's Lydia," she said when Sarah answered. "Tyler and I are heading to the mainland soon. Can you recommend someplace safe where we can ride out the storm?"

"Oh, Lydia." Sarah sounded stressed. No doubt the approaching storm had her troubled. "I wish you could follow us, but I'm driving straight to my parent's house. Bobby and I are leaving Rob."

From her tone of voice, something more than a storm was brewing at the Jackson house. "Leaving? You mean because of the storm?"

"I wish that's all it was. Look, I can't talk now. But if you and Tyler head west, you'll eventually get to Interstate 95 and the motels. You'll be safe there. I promise to call when Bobby and I are settled."

"Is there anything I can do?"

Sarah sighed. "Pray for us, Lydia."

If only she could.

Atlanta traffic snarled through the city at a pace that tried Matt's patience. Two lanes closed for road repair had turned the city's interstate into gridlock.

Matt picked up his phone. He had called Roger Harris earlier to set up an appointment with the chief of police. Because of the traffic delays, he wouldn't make the scheduled meeting.

"Roger, it's Matt. I'm hung up in traffic coming

into the city. Can you relay that to the chief? See if I can move the meeting back thirty minutes or so."

"Will do."

By the time Matt arrived at police headquarters, he felt as though he'd been pounded in the gut with a baseball bat from the frustration eating a hole in his stomach. He needed to deliver his information and head back to Sanctuary. Lydia and Tyler were still in danger, and with the encroaching storm, the island might have to be evacuated. This wasn't the day for him to be lollygagging in Atlanta.

Harris greeted him when he stepped into the office. "The chief's not here. There's an emergency at Lenox Square. Doubt he'll be back at headquarters before the end of the day."

"Then tell me how to get to Lenox?"

"No can do, buddy. He won't be dealing with anyone or anything except the current issue until tomorrow at the earliest. White powder and a large amount of it. It's got the city spooked. Hazmat did an initial test and found it positive for anthrax."

"Yeah, and how often are they wrong?" Matt's irritation was evident in his voice. "You know those initial tests are too sensitive. Didn't you have something over at Fort McPherson a few years ago? Hazmat said it was a sure thing, then twenty-four hours later, the CDC gives the all clear."

Harris let out a breath. "I hear you. But that still won't get you in to see the chief." Harris held out his hand. "Give me the file. I'll make sure he sees it once the emergency passes."

Matt wanted to discuss the information with the Chief and no one else. "You ever have any dealings with the Men's Club?"

"Not me."

"How about Paris?"

"Yeah, he was working that arson case."

"That's what I was afraid of," Matt said.

Lydia's contact hadn't been sure of the dirty cop's name. Matt had worked with Harris in Miami. Six years and not a blemish on the man's record.

Everything told him Harris wasn't involved, but he wouldn't do anything to endanger Lydia and Tyler.

"The file can wait. Tell the chief to call me when the anthrax scare is over."

Anxious to get back to Sanctuary before the storm hit, Matt hastened to his pickup, slid into the driver's side and dropped the printout on the seat next to him. Grabbing his car phone, he dialed the cell he'd given Lydia.

"The chief was tied up with a possible anthrax scare," Matt said when she answered.

"Did you leave the information?"

"I couldn't. Not that I think Harris is involved. But you and Tyler are too important to me to take a chance by divulging your whereabouts or the evidence Sonny hid."

"Oh, Matt," she sighed.

"I'll return to Atlanta after the storm passes and

when the chief's free. He'll get the names, just a few days later than I planned. How's Tyler?"

"Right now, he's eating oatmeal cookies and watching a DVD."

"And the weather?"

"Raining. The wind's picked up a bit. I managed to fasten the shutters on all the windows. We'll leave as soon as I cover the sliding door to the deck."

"You need to get off the island now, Lydia."

"When I finish."

"Leave it. Your safety's more important than the house. Katherine would tell you the same thing."

"It'll only take me a few minutes."

Matt hung up with worry gnawing in his gut. He tapped in the number to security headquarters. No answer. The call automatically forwarded to Eunice.

"How's the weather?" he asked.

"Getting worse. The water's rising. The guys are notifying the residents of a possible evacuation."

"Contact Jason. Tell him to head over to 50 Cove Road. That woman who moved into Katherine O'Connor's house needs help."

"Any idea when you'll be back in the area?"

"ASAP, Eunice. Keep me posted."

Matt closed his cell and turned the key in the ignition. Nothing.

He tried again.

The truck was only a year old and top-of-the-line. No reason to have a problem and way too early to need a new battery.

Grumbling, he climbed out and raised the hood.
Oh, yeah, he had a problem. A big one.
Someone had yanked out the fuel pump relay.

TWENTY

Lydia raised the first of the two storm shutters to the sliding-glass door and slipped it into place. Wiping the rain from her face, she adjusted the hood on her coat and reached for the second shutter.

Tyler stuck his head out the door.

"Stay inside, honey. I don't want you to get wet."

"Mom, there's a man at the front door."

"Who is it?"

Tyler shrugged, a worried look wrapped around his small face.

"Get your slicker. We'll leave in a few minutes."

Glancing around the corner of the house, Lydia spied a pickup parked in the front drive with the familiar security logo on the door.

"Matt—"

She stepped forward before realizing the person peering through the front door peephole wasn't Matt.

"May I help you?" she called over the rising wind.

The guy twirled around, seemingly caught off guard.

"Matt phoned Eunice. Said you were still on the island. I'm Butch Griffin with security."

Lydia remembered the young woman she had met at Matt's office. "You're Natalie's dad. Thanks for coming over." She pointed toward the back of the house. "I've got one last shutter to slip into place. Mind giving me a hand?"

Butch shook his head. "No way, lady. We've got a mandatory island evacuation."

"But—"

"The water's rising. Your car won't make it across the mainland road. I'll have to drive you out."

"I didn't think it had gotten that bad."

"Leave everything. Let's go."

"My son's in the house."

Butch nodded. "Get the boy. We'll take my truck."

Lydia hastened inside and glanced at the boarded-up windows. Hopefully Katherine's home would survive the storm. Lydia pulled the heavy curtain over the sliding door. If only the uncovered safety glass would withstand the raging wind.

The house seemed eerily dark as she grabbed Tyler's slicker. She could care less about their few possessions. The important thing was keeping Tyler safe.

She glanced at the oil painting on the wall depicting Christ on the Sea of Galilee.

You protected the disciples from the storm. Now protect us.

Butch entered the house and stood in front of Katherine's curio cabinet, eyeing the figurines.

"That man scares me, Mom," Tyler whispered as she guided his arms into the slicker. "I pushed the alarm."

"You did what?"

"The silent warning. Remember Chief said to tap in the code if a bad man was outside? I sent Matt the signal."

"Honey, Mr. Griffin is here to help us. Besides, Matt's in Atlanta. He won't be back for a few more hours."

Lydia didn't know how to cancel the alarm. Not wanting to cause more trouble, she decided not to tell Butch about Tyler's rash mistake.

The rain pounded them as Lydia helped Tyler into the truck and scooted in next to him.

"I called Eunice," Butch said, climbing into the driver's seat. "Mainland road's already flooded. We'll head to the marina. There's a boat that'll take care of you."

His choice of words sent goose bumps scurrying along her arms. Evidently, Eunice hadn't mentioned the silent alarm.

At the end of the driveway, Griffin turned north toward the marina.

Lydia pulled Tyler close. He felt warm. "Does your tummy hurt, honey?"

"No, but my head does," he admitted.

She dropped her cheek to his forehead. "You've got a fever."

"There's a hospital on the mainland, if the kid's sick," Butch said.

Probably just a twenty-four hour virus, but after Tyler's harrowing experience in the rip current, she'd feel better having a doctor look him over. If Tyler had aspirated water, something more serious might set in. Butch was right. They could get medical help once they reached the mainland.

Rain pounded the car. The windshield wipers struggled to keep up with the deluge.

Lydia strained to see the road. "Whose boat are we taking?"

"Neighbor of yours. Jackson."

"Bobby's dad? I thought he already left the island."

Butch snorted. "Wife and kid got out by car. Jackson wanted to take his boat."

Lydia drew Tyler closer. Whatever problems Sarah and Rob were experiencing, Lydia knew she could count on Rob to get them safely to the mainland.

At the marina, the wind whipped off the ocean, sending sprays of water flying over the dock. The gray sky grew even darker as Lydia and Tyler crawled out of the truck.

Tyler tugged on her arm. "Mom, look."

He pointed to the far side of the parking lot where a lone car sat parked.

A black Mercedes.

Lydia adjusted the hood on Tyler's slicker to keep the rain off his face. "It's okay, honey. Lots of people have that type of car."

Griffin nudged her forward. "Hurry, you two. The water's rising."

Taking Tyler's hand, she guided him toward the large boat at the end of the pier. Even to her less than nautical eyes, the high-powered craft appeared seaworthy.

She'd be glad when she saw her neighbor. A friendly face would ease her concern.

Rob came out on deck as they approached, his face strained. Stepping onto the dock, he picked Tyler up and carried him onto the boat. Griffin and Lydia followed.

"Thanks so much," she said once they were in the cabin. Protected from the storm's fury, she felt a sense of relief. She led Tyler to a small couch, sloughed out of her wet raincoat and helped Tyler take his off, then sat next to him.

"Tyler's got a fever, Rob. He needs to see a doctor."

"The storm's moving in fast. We've got to get underway. We'll talk later."

Tyler rested his head on Lydia's shoulder and closed his eyes. The heat from his body burned against her.

Lydia laid Tyler on the couch and climbed the steps to the bridge. Surely, Rob had a first-aid kit on board with something to combat fever.

Sheltering her eyes with her right hand, she held on to the stair railing thankful for the canopy that buffered the wind and rain.

She glanced around. The boat was headed away from the mainland.

"Aren't we going the wrong direction?" she called out over the sound of the powerful engine and the waves slapping against the craft.

Rob turned to glare at her. "Get below, Lydia."

She pointed to the large gray forms rising in the distance. "Those are the boulders by Katherine's house."

Griffin grabbed Lydia's arm.

"Take her below," Rob ordered. "Watch both of them."

"Let go of me," she demanded.

Griffin shoved her toward the cabin. She pulled her arm free and glared up at Rob. "What's going on?"

"Tying up loose ends, Lydia."

"I…I don't understand."

"Your husband didn't understand, either."

She gasped. "You knew Sonny?"

"I know most of the people who work at my club."

"*Your* club?"

"Sonny liked the rich life, the big homes and fancy cars. Of course, when he realized the club was involved in diverse activities, we had a parting of the ways."

"He came to Sanctuary to see you," she said, everything falling into place. "Is Joel involved, as well?"

"Not that wimp." Rob laughed. "Sonny came down to help me with a special Web project. A few weeks later, he tells me his aunt is looking at property on the island. Guess he figured one of these days the old broad would die, and he'd inherit the house. Setting himself up for the future."

"The black Mercedes. That's your car." Lydia glared at Rob. "When Sonny wanted out, you killed him."

Rob glanced at Griffin. "Talk to my man, Butch."

She whipped around to look at the security guard. "You set the fire in my house."

"Just following orders from the boss." Griffin's shirtsleeve rose as he pointed to Rob, exposing an A.P. digital watch.

"You tried to grab Tyler in the school yard," Lydia gasped. "Which one of you broke into Katherine's home?"

"You made it easy for me," Rob said. "The sliding-glass door wasn't locked."

"But the alarm—"

"Bobby saw Tyler punch in the code." He smiled. "Kids can be so helpful."

He glanced down into the cabin where Tyler slept. "Your boy said his dad had given him a high-tech toy. What better place for a computer geek to hide the evidence. I checked all the discs. Nothing."

Rob pursed his lips. "Did a little nosing around while I was there. Made sure there was no evidence to worry about. After I get rid of you and Tyler, the police will shut the book on Sonny Sloan and family. They'll think you set the fire, instead of Griffin." He looked at his accomplice. "Mr. Pyro Man, we call him."

Butch bared his teeth. "Fire can be used in so many ways. Even for a guy who needed to be silenced in jail."

"What do you mean?" Lydia pressed.

Rob shook his head. "Somebody did a little work for me and saw more than he should have. Said he was going to talk. That was the last thing he said. By the way, you should close your curtains at night, Lydia."

She remembered the Peeping Tom's face—Rob's face—at the window.

The jagged boulders loomed ahead.

"If you're going to start a fire in Katherine's house, the police won't buy it," Lydia insisted. "Two arson cases would raise anyone's suspicions."

"We've got other plans for you," Butch sneered. "Although I can add fire to the mix, if you like."

"Matt will find us." Lydia hoped her voice sounded more convincing to them than it did to her.

Rob shook his head. "He's having a little trouble with his truck in Atlanta. I wouldn't count on him."

The boat slowed. Rob cut the engine.

"Get your boy. Tell him you're going for a ride."

Butch lowered a dinghy over the side.

Lydia's heart beat against her chest. Frantically, she searched for a way out. "We won't make it in this storm."

Rob bowed mockingly. "Then I'll have Butch escort you."

"Let Tyler stay on board, Rob. He's so sick. He won't tell the police anything."

"Get below." Butch pushed her forward.

She stumbled down the steps and into the cabin. Her right hand brushed against her skirt.

Her fingers touched the cell phone Matt had given her.

Sitting on the couch next to Tyler, she inched the phone from her pocket.

"Honey, you have to wake up." She kissed Tyler

on the forehead. Keeping the phone hidden from Butch's view, she pushed 9-1-1 and Send.

"Where are you taking us?" She directed her voice toward the mouthpiece.

Dear Lord, let someone answer.

"To the caves. They'll never find you there," Butch said behind her.

"The boulders by Katherine O'Connor's house on Sanctuary Island?"

If only her voice could be heard over the roar of the storm. She jammed the phone between the cushions and pulled Tyler into her arms.

Keep transmitting.

Butch shoved them up the steps.

Rob grabbed Tyler.

His bottom lip quivered. "Mama?" He started to cry.

Black water churned around them. The storm howled and waves rocked the boat.

"Get in the dinghy," Butch ordered, his hand tight on her arm as he forced her over the side.

Lydia's foot slipped. Her left leg plunged into the cold water. Butch shoved her into the bottom of the tiny craft. She landed on her left arm. Pain sliced along her shoulder.

Tears clouded her eyes. Terrified the dinghy would capsize, she was more afraid of what would happen once they were in the cave.

"Keep Tyler with you, Rob," she pleaded.

"No, Mama," her son screamed.

The neighbor laughed.

Butch climbed into the dinghy and pulled a rope from his pocket. "Hands behind your back."

She didn't move.

He slapped her. She reeled from the blow.

"Do what I say. Now!"

He grabbed her arms and wrenched them back. She gasped in pain. The cord cut into her wrists as he pulled it tight.

"Mama." Tyler cried.

Rob bound her son's hands, then handed him down to Butch.

"Take care of them. I'll wait here."

Tyler huddled next to her, sobs racking his small body. She leaned close, trying to protect him from the rain and wind.

Butch rowed them toward a black hole in the rock, then turned on a searchlight, illuminating the craggy interior of a vast cave.

Lydia's stomach roiled. At the far end, an outcrop of rock hung about six feet above the water.

Butch guided the boat to the raised landing. He forced Lydia and Tyler out of the boat and pushed them up the steep incline and onto the ledge while he followed.

"Don't leave us here." Lydia cried in desperation.

She looked at the opening of the cave. The sea level rose with each lap of water. The entrance would soon be covered.

"No one'll find you." Butch laughed. "Not even your boyfriend, Matt."

He stooped to gather an armful of dry twigs from under a nearby overhang.

Fear wrapped around her. "What are you doing with that driftwood?"

"You know I love fire. My signature, so to speak." He forced them back-to-back, tied them together and arranged the twigs at their feet.

"Kind of appropriate to die like your husband, don't you think? 'Course he pleaded with me. Said for me to take him but not hurt you two."

Griffin pulled a lighter from his pocket, held it to the dry kindling and fanned the smoldering wood.

"You can't leave us here," Lydia cried as the fire ignited.

"Just watch me." He climbed down from the ledge and into the dinghy then rowed across the choppy water.

"Happy camping," he called back to them. His evil laughter echoed in the cave as he passed through the entrance.

Lydia scooted back, pushing Tyler clear of the flickering flames. The glow from the fire illuminated the tomb that surrounded them. She searched the rocks. Even if they weren't tied up, there'd be no way to escape.

"Mama?" Tyler shivered, nudging her.

"I love you, honey."

Cold steel touched her hand.

"Dad's knife," Tyler said. "I got it when you were on the phone."

He jammed it into her outstretched palm.

She grabbed for the knife, felt it slip between her fingers. Catching it, she worked it around in her hand.

Let it open.

Digging her fingernail into the groove of the blade, she tugged. Her nail broke. She tried again.

The flames darted along the kindling. Smoke drifted upward. Her eyes burned. She tasted the acrid ash. Just like the fire seven months ago.

Heat seared her legs. She tried to inch away from the flames.

Once again, her fingers pried at the knife.

Please, God. Help me.

The blade opened.

She grabbed Tyler's hands.

"Hold still, honey."

Rob had wrapped the rope only once around his small wrists. She worked the blade back and forth, hoping she wouldn't nick his flesh.

The rope fell free.

Without prompting, Tyler reached down and untied his feet, then kicked at the twigs, the fire licking Lydia's legs.

Oblivious to her burns, she turned the sharp blade to her own hands. Pain slashed her finger.

"Mom, you're bleeding."

"Take the knife. Cut the rope for me."

Tyler grabbed the handle.

"Saw back and forth," she told him.

Tyler's small fingers shook, but he worked rapidly. At last, he cut through the thick hemp.

Taking the knife from him, she bent down and severed the rope binding her legs.

Finally free, she slumped with relief and wrapped her arms around his shivering body. Light from the last burning branches cast an eerie glow across the pool of water.

As she watched, the water rose another inch, covering the cave's entrance.

They were trapped.

TWENTY-ONE

Matt arranged for his truck to be towed to a nearby Atlanta garage for repairs and signed for a loaner car.

Once he hit I-75 South, he floored the accelerator. With the anthrax scare at Lenox Square, the streets should be clear of cops. He didn't want to waste time explaining why he was doing ninety in a fifty-five-miles-per-hour speed zone.

Outside the city, he called Eunice.

"What's the latest?"

"The storm's turned, heading straight for Sanctuary. The island's under evacuation. Water's rising and the Bay Road's near flood level."

"What about Lydia Sloan and her son?"

"Butch went out there earlier."

"Butch?"

"Everyone else was tied up with the evacuation, Chief."

"Are they headed for the mainland?"

"Haven't heard," Eunice said.

"I'll phone the O'Connor house."

"Doubt you'll get through. The island phone service went out about fifteen minutes ago. I had a silent alarm from that residence a while back."

Matt's pulse raced as fast as the autos along the highway. "When?"

"Not long after Butch left. 'Spect they tapped in the security code and hit the wrong buttons." Eunice sighed. "You know how often *that* happens."

Did Lydia inadvertently send the alarm when she punched in the regular code? Or was she sending him a warning?

Matt didn't like it. He'd given Lydia and Tyler thorough instruction on the silent alarm. Both of them understood the system. Perhaps the storm had scared Tyler and the kid cried wolf.

Matt shook his head. Butch wasn't the friendliest. Not by a long shot. If he'd done anything to frighten them—

"You want me to call Jason's cell?" Eunice's voice pulled Matt back to the issue at hand. "Have him check on Ms. O'Connor's houseguests?"

"No, I will. You phone Sam Snyder. Ask him to meet me at the mainland marina with that motorboat of his."

"Water's pretty rough for a ride, Chief."

"By the time I arrive, it may be the only way to the island. Explain the situation to Sam. Tell him I need to get back to Sanctuary."

Matt hung up and tried the cell he'd given Lydia. The voice mail clicked on.

"Lydia, it's Matt. Call me back."

He disconnected and called Jason.

"How's it look on the island?"

"Storm's heading our way. Evacuation's in progress. Residents are cooperating. No problems so far."

"Have you seen Lydia Sloan?"

"Katherine's houseguest?" Jason asked.

"Yeah. Eunice said Butch's helping her. Should be off the island by now. Check her house, and let me know if you see anything contrary."

"Roger. Out."

Matt disconnected and studied the sky. Dark clouds filled the horizon. The wind had picked up speed and the temperature had dropped significantly.

Ten minutes later, his phone rang.

"Chief, it's Jason. Natalie just called. She's in labor and needs a ride to the hospital. I'm headed that way."

"Where's Griffin?"

"I saw him boarding Rob Jackson's boat down at the marina. Ms. Sloan and her boy in tow. I wanted to tell Butch about Natalie. Only I didn't get there in time."

Matt let out a sigh of relief. "Rob's probably docked at the mainland by now."

"No, sir," Jason responded. "He was aimed in the other direction."

Where would Jackson be going in the midst of a storm? Back to Katherine's?

A slash of fear cut through him.

"Jason, backtrack to the O'Connor place. See where they dropped anchor…Jason?"

No answer.

"Jason, you hear me?"

Matt's phone beeped.

Call disconnected.

Frantically, Matt hit Memory for the dispatcher.

No answer from Eunice.

He redialed Jason. A message flashed.

Call failed.

The storm was in full fury when Matt arrived at the marina and found Sam and his motorboat.

"Stay here," Matt yelled above the howling wind. "I don't want to put you in danger, Sam."

The old guy shook his head. "Don't leave me out of the action. Plus you'll need another pair of hands. Climb aboard."

Even with two large spotlights flashing through the night, visibility was poor. Waves battered the boat, but Sam was an accomplished seaman and kept them on course.

The boulders appeared in the distance.

"Flash the lights over the rocks, would you, Sam?"

"Highest tide surge I've ever seen." Sam squinted into the angry squall. "Even the entrances to the caves are covered."

Something caught Matt's eye.

"See that?" He pointed to the crest of the boulder. "Looks like smoke."

Sam scratched his head. Another wisp escaped

from the rock. "You know these rocks always fascinated Rob."

"Pull up a bit," Matt said.

Sam edged the boat near the jagged peaks.

"Give me as much light as you can."

Matt leaped onto the boulder and climbed straight up to the ledge. Might be a long shot, but the caves were a perfect place to hide someone. Or leave someone to die.

"Lydia," he screamed, knowing his voice was lost in the wind. She would never hear him over the roar of the angry storm.

Where was the smoke coming from? He signaled Sam to shine the spotlight on top of the boulder again. Nothing.

Matt shielded his eyes from the onslaught of rain. One more puff of smoke, and he'd be able to pinpoint its origination.

There. A tiny whiff curled skyward before it vanished in the wind and rain.

He gave Sam a thumbs-up and raced forward, spying a fissure in the rock. He peered down. The glow from a dying fire illuminated the cave below.

Lydia and Tyler stood huddled on a small outcrop of rock. His initial elation at finding them crashed.

Water lapped over the ledge.

He blinked. The tiny fire went out.

Lydia and Tyler were cast into total darkness.

TWENTY-TWO

Lydia shivered with fear as she hugged Tyler, his body on fire with fever. She pulled him into the light from the burning twigs. His eyes stared back at her, dull, lifeless, glistening like a sheet of ice.

Tyler slumped against her. So small. So frail.

The light flickered. Before long they'd be plunged into darkness.

Her heart broke when she thought of her son's life cut short. It didn't matter about her own. Nothing mattered, except Tyler.

Oh, God, why have You forsaken us?

She looked into the water—a dark abyss that rose ever so steadily.

Even if they could swim to the entrance, the rough seas outside the cave would crash them against the rocks. They'd never make shore.

She hugged her child tighter. The end was close. The water would rise and…

The last glowing ember went out.

Darkness.

Tyler moaned, wrapping his arms around her waist. "Shh, baby. Shh."

Lydia looked up toward the heavens. She and Tyler needed a miracle. She closed her eyes.

Don't turn Your back on me, Lord. Save my son. He's too young to die.

"Lydia."

Her eyes blinked open. Now, she was hearing voices.

She patted Tyler's back and rubbed her hand over his shoulders.

"Lydia."

Her heart lunged in her chest. "Matt?"

"Look up."

She tilted her head back and studied the roof of the cave. All she saw was darkness.

"Turn the boat's spotlight this way, Sam." She heard Matt shout.

A ray of light flickered through a fissure in the ceiling of the cave.

"Matt, we're stuck. Get Sam to bring his boat," she screamed.

"The water's covered the entrance."

"Then swim in to us."

"I'd never find the opening in time. There's only one way. You've got to swim out, Lydia."

"Tyler's burning with fever. He won't make it."

"You've got to try. Have Tyler wrap his arms around your back. Dog paddle across the cave. Sam's positioning a searchlight toward that section of the rocks. You should be able to see the light underwater. It'll show you the way out."

Lydia shook her head, her fear of being submerged as strong as her fear of dying.

"I…I can't, Matt."

"It's the only way you can save Tyler."

"You know I can't go under water."

"Tell him to hold on to your shoulders. Paddle with your hands and kick your feet. When you get close to the entrance, duck your head under water. Your body will follow. You'll be submerged for only a short time, a minute at most. I'll meet you on the other side."

Tears streamed down her face. Matt was asking too much.

"Mama, I'm scared." Tyler cried.

"Trust me," Matt yelled. "You can do it."

Trust. There it was again.

"I trust you, Matt. But I can't trust myself."

"Ask God to swim with you, Lydia. God helped me save Tyler from the rip current. He'll guide you through the entrance."

Lydia's heart broke. Her son shouldn't have to die in this dark cave because his mother didn't have the courage to save him.

Matt believed in her. She had to believe in herself. And even more important, she had to believe in God.

Jesus, I trust in You.

She knelt on the ledge. The water swirled around her.

"Climb on my back, Tyler. Mama's going to swim us out."

"I'm cold." He moaned.

"I know, honey. But we've got to get to Matt."

She turned so Tyler could wrap his hands around her shoulders. "Hold on tight."

She lowered herself into the chilly water.

The spotlight from Sam's boat flickered in the distance, the opening to the cave about three feet below the surface.

"We're going to paddle across the water, then we'll dive below. Like a dolphin, Tyler. You've got to hold your breath when I tell you. Remember your swimming lessons?"

She could feel Tyler nod his head.

"Don't let go."

Slowly, she paddled toward the far side of the cave. Her left shoulder ached where she'd hit the dinghy.

"Tyler, suck in a big breath. Hold it until we're out of the cave. One, two, three. Now."

Lydia grabbed a lungful of air and dove below the surface.

The memories returned. She was a young child trapped in the waves. Panic seized her.

Jesus, I trust in You.

She opened her eyes and saw the entrance outlined with a glowing light.

Tyler slipped. She grasped his hands.

If only he'd wrap his legs around my waist. Tell him what to do, Lord.

Instantly, his legs circled her.

Once he was secure, she dived deeper and entered the opening.

Froth from the angry surf bubbled around them, like when she was a child.

She struggled. Tried to kick through the opening.

Jagged rocks surrounded them. Something tugged against her foot. She tried to pull free. Her leg caught.

Suddenly, Matt was beside her in the water. She unlocked Tyler's hands from around her neck and shoved her child into his outstretched arms.

Matt kicked to the surface, carrying Tyler to safety. The current pushed her against the submerged boulders, her arms scraping the rough stone.

She yanked her foot but couldn't free herself.

What held her? She looked down, peering through the murky water.

The rope still tied around her ankle was caught on a rock.

She shoved her hand in her pocket and pulled out the knife. It slipped from her fingers and dropped to the rocks below.

Her lungs burned. Fatigue overwhelmed her.

Tyler was safe. Matt had saved him. That's all that mattered. Matt would take care of Tyler. She didn't need to worry. She closed her eyes. All she wanted to do was sleep....

Matt broke the surface of the water with Tyler in his arms. He handed the boy to Sam and dived back down for Lydia.

What happened? She had almost cleared the entrance when he took Tyler from her. But she never surfaced.

He swam deeper.

Overhead, Sam adjusted the beam of light.

There, Matt saw her. Her body hung suspended in the water.

Matt spied the rope, grabbed it and tugged.

The rope held.

He yanked again. No change.

Wrapping his arms around Lydia, he spied something on the rock below.

A knife.

Thank You, Lord.

He cut the rope and kicked, breaking the surface, her limp body in his arms.

"Take her, Sam," he called out, lifting her into the boat.

Matt climbed in, knelt beside her and felt her carotid artery. No pulse.

Opening her mouth, he checked for an obstruction.

"Head for the mainland, Sam. Radio the sheriff's office. Tell them we'll need an ambulance."

He cupped his mouth over hers and blew. Her chest rose ever so slightly. Two more quick breaths.

He felt for her sternum, fisted his hands and pushed down. "One and two and three..."

The storm raged. Rain pelted them. The wind howled. Waves splashed against the boat.

Over and over again, he pushed air into her lungs, willing her to live.

"Mama." Tyler cried, huddled in the corner of the boat. "Don't die, Mama."

The sound of the boy's pleas broke Matt's heart. He couldn't lose Lydia. He told her she'd make it to safety. She trusted him.

"Lydia," Matt screamed over the wail of the wind, knowing all was lost.

TWENTY-THREE

Matt stood in the hallway of the pediatric intensive care unit and stared through the glass window. Tyler looked pale as death.

A nurse checked the ventilator humming next to the boy's bed. A tube ran into Tyler's nose, sending oxygen to his body—oxygen he needed desperately but his lungs weren't able to provide.

Matt's heart hung heavy in his chest. Pneumonia, the doctors had said when they arrived by ambulance at the hospital. The boy's temperature had hovered at 105 degrees, causing him to shake uncontrollably. The doctors gave him a twenty-five percent chance of surviving. If he made it through the first twelve hours, the odds would double in his favor.

Matt felt a hand on his shoulder. He turned to see Wayne Turner.

"What a night," the mainland sheriff said.

"And it's not over yet." Matt glanced back at the small child struggling to live.

"How's the little guy?"

"Fighting hard." Matt swallowed the lump that had taken residence in his throat ever since they had arrived at the hospital.

"Savannah law enforcement arrested Jackson and Griffin," Turner said.

Matt turned to face the mainland chief. "Now that's good news."

"Seems Lydia managed to make a 9-1-1 call. The operator heard the distress in her voice. He kept the line open. Once you notified us of the situation, we were able to track down the boat, using the signal from the cell. Seems Jackson thought they could escape up the coast to Savannah. Coast guard picked them up."

"What about the situation in Atlanta?" Matt asked.

"That late night call you made to the chief of police paid off. He pulled Roger Harris in, wanted to know why Harris hadn't told him about your visit. Seems Harris was involved from the start and had something to do with that Miami situation that killed your partner."

"Rodriquez?"

"Harris tipped off the Miami drug ring that your partner was on to them. They were waiting for him."

Matt had trusted Harris in Miami and then again in Atlanta. And Harris had recommended Griffin, who had been involved in the Men's Club from the beginning.

"Another interesting fact," the sheriff continued. "The guy who killed your partner—"

"Ricky Gallegos?"

"That's right. Seems Jackson worked with him.

Gave the police enough evidence to nail the guy. They hauled Gallegos in for questioning about an hour ago. Looks like they'll put him away for life."

Relief swept over Matt. The Miami case was closed. Harris had set Rodriquez up. If Matt had answered his cell and joined his partner, he would have seen the same fate as Pete.

"What about the people Sonny named in the Web site?"

"They're being questioned. My guys are searching the O'Connor house. Funny, her home didn't have any damage. Jackson's house next door was leveled by the storm."

Before Matt could comment, the sheriff's cell phone rang. He pulled it to his ear, grunted a few words back to the caller and hung up.

"More good news. Seems Tyler threw a disc away."

"Probably from his Action-Pac," Matt said. "His dad gave him the toy the night of the fire."

"The disc must not have worked so the kid tossed it. Luckily, we found it in the bottom of his trash can. Plugged it into a computer and hit the jackpot—enough information on the Men's Club and the associated operations to nail everyone involved." Wayne slapped Matt's back. "Keep me posted on the boy's progress."

The sheriff walked down the hall just as the doctor slipped into Tyler's room. He checked the bedside monitor and listened to the child's lungs.

Matt's chest tightened. He closed his eyes, afraid of what the doc would find.

When he looked up, he was filled with relief.

Tyler's eyes blinked open. The doctor smiled and gave Matt a thumbs-up.

The nurse stayed at the boy's bedside while the doctor stepped into the hallway. "He's a strong kid. He'll be breathing on his own in no time. His temp's still elevated but his white count has come down."

The doctor put his hand on Matt's shoulder. "That's a good sign, Chief. Means the antibiotics are controlling the infection. Give him a day or two, and we'll have to hold him down."

Smiling for the first time since the storm, Matt headed for the elevator. On the second floor, he stopped at Room 225 and stepped into the darkness.

"Good news," he said.

Lydia lay on the hospital bed, her legs bandaged, her face splotched with tears. She looked up with expectation. "Tyler?"

"His infection's better. The pediatrician said he's going to pull through."

Tears welled up in her eyes. *"Thank You, Lord."*

She grabbed Matt's hand. "When can I see him?"

"We'll ask your doctor when he makes rounds."

Matt stroked her cheek. "Last night I thought I lost you, then Tyler's pneumonia. I prayed so hard. I was afraid I'd lose both of you."

She squeezed his hand. "You saved us, Matt."

He shook his head. "You were the one who swam Tyler to safety."

"And then I got hung up on the rocks. If you hadn't been there, we both would have drowned."

"We're a good team." He smiled down at her. "Maybe we should team up on a permanent basis."

She laughed through her tears. "Is that what I think it sounds like?"

"If you mean a proposal, that's it exactly. I've got a pickup and enough stuff to fit in the truck bed. Not big on possessions, but I've got a heart overflowing with love for you and Tyler."

"That's all we need."

He squeezed her hand. "Katherine sends her love. I talked to her a few hours ago."

"And her house?"

"Made it safely through the storm. Jackson's wasn't so lucky."

"Fate?"

"More like divine justice."

He reached in his pocket and pulled out the knife. He handed it to her. Sonny's name was engraved on the handle. "God works in mysterious ways."

She took the knife and studied it. "Butch said the night he burned our house, Sonny was worried about us. Maybe he did love us, after all."

Matt rubbed her hand. "I love you, Lydia."

She smiled as he lowered his lips to hers.

The sun peeked over the horizon. A new day dawned. A very bright new day.

EPILOGUE

Matt held Lydia's arm and helped her up the steps of the Community Church. The burns on her legs had almost healed. Tyler waved at Chase Davenport when they entered the sanctuary and slipped into a pew.

Matt nudged Lydia and discreetly pointed to the opposite side of the church where Natalie sat holding her infant daughter. Jason cooed at the baby, his arm around Natalie.

"Looks like they're trying to straighten out the past," Matt whispered in her ear.

Lydia smiled, happy to see the couple together. Turning to face her son, she brushed Tyler's hair out of his eyes and hugged him close.

"When's Bobby coming to visit?" he asked.

"Next Sunday, honey." Right arm around Tyler, she reached her left hand out to Matt.

He rubbed his fingers over hers, the diamond engagement ring sparkling in the light.

If Jason and Natalie set a date, the Community Church would see two weddings in the near future.

Lydia turned as Katherine walked down the aisle on the arm of an elderly gentleman.

Make that three weddings.

Katherine and her Irish beau were as giddy as schoolkids. The older couple spied Lydia and waved before they settled into a pew.

"Turn to page 105 in your songbooks," the organist announced as the service began. "'Give Thanks To The Lord With All Your Heart.'"

Yes, Lord, so much for which to be thankful. A man to love, my beautiful son and our new home in Sanctuary. But most of all, thank You for allowing me to be secure in Your love. I can now say without reservation, Jesus, I trust in You.

* * * * *

Watch for Debby Giusti's next
Love Inspired Suspense, on sale August 2007.
You'll keep the lights on for
SCARED TO DEATH!

Dear Reader,

No matter how strong our faith, often the first inclination when problems arise is to wonder whether the Lord will hear our cry for help. If we're under undue stress, prayer can be difficult, and sometimes just a few simple words may be all we can manage.

When all seems lost in *Nowhere To Hide,* Lydia remembers the words stitched on the sampler: "Jesus, I trust in you." As she repeats that little prayer, she puts her trust in the Lord and finds the strength to save her son.

Those same words have helped me through difficult times, bringing me peace and a confidence that the Lord is in control. If you're facing problems, I hope you'll turn to the Lord. He is the sure foundation who will never let us down.

Thank you for reading my debut novel. My second Love Inspired Suspense book, *Scared to Death,* will be in bookstores this August. Be sure to visit me online at www.debbygiusti.com and write me at debby@debbygiusti.com.

Wishing you abundant blessings,

Debby Giusti

QUESTIONS FOR DISCUSSION

1. The title *Nowhere To Hide* has both a metaphorical and literal meaning. How is the island a place of sanctuary for both Lydia and Matt? From what or whom are they trying to hide? When we try to hide from the Lord, we know He seeks us out. How is that especially true for Lydia?

2. Lydia allowed her relationships with her father and husband to adversely affect her relationship with God. Have there been times in your life when problems with family or friends changed the way you felt about the Lord? How were you able to move beyond those problems?

3. Like Lydia, sometimes we find it hard to trust. What are some of the reasons in your own life that keep you from trusting completely? How can a loving church community help you open your heart to Jesus?

4. Matt feels responsible for his partner's death. He can't forgive himself and feels the Lord can't forgive him, either. What happens in the story that allows Matt to accept the Lord's forgiveness? Why is it so hard to forgive ourselves?

5. The painting of Jesus calming the sea and the cross-stitched sampler serve as visual reminders to Lydia of a God in whom she *can* put her trust. What do you have in your home that reminds you of the Lord?

6. Katherine and Connie are women of faith and serve as Christian role models for Lydia and Matt. Have there been strong Christians in your life who have been examples to you in times of need? Or have you been that solid foundation to someone facing a difficult situation? Discuss.

7. Lydia fears water because of what happened in her childhood. Matt encourages her to learn to swim, knowing that if she faces her fear, she'll be able to control its hold on her. Do you believe Matt's advice is sound? Do you have an example that shows how you faced and eventually conquered your own fear?

8. Lydia turns to God to overcome her fear of water and save her son. When has the Lord helped you overcome a seemingly insurmountable obstacle? How did you find the courage and strength to persevere?

9. What is the turning point in Matt and Lydia's relationship? When does Lydia start to trust Matt and why?

10. At the end of the book, Lydia sees Sonny's name on the pocketknife. Why is the knife important? Do you think Lydia was able to forgive her husband?

Celebrate Love Inspired's 10th anniversary
with top authors and great stories all year long!

SUSPENSE
RIVETING INSPIRATIONAL ROMANCE

THE SECRETS OF STONELEY

**Six sisters face murder, mayhem and mystery
while unraveling the past.**

Deadly Payoff
VALERIE HANSEN

**Book 5 of the multiauthor
The Secrets of Stoneley
miniseries.**

Delia Blanchard was still
recovering from learning that
the woman shot to death in
the library was not her mother
when she got a second shock.
Her former love Shaun Murphy
was hired to repair the damage
after the shooting. Had she
been given a second chance?

***Available May 2007
wherever you
buy books.***

Steeple
Hill®

REQUEST YOUR FREE BOOKS!
2 FREE RIVETING INSPIRATIONAL NOVELS
PLUS 2 FREE MYSTERY GIFTS

Love Inspired®

SUSPENSE

YES! Please send me 2 FREE Love Inspired® Suspense novels and my 2 FREE mystery gifts. After receiving them, if I don't wish to receive any more books, I can return the shipping statement marked "cancel." If I don't cancel, I will receive 4 brand-new novels every month and be billed just $3.99 per book in the U.S. or $4.74 per book in Canada, plus 25¢ shipping and handling per book and applicable taxes, if any*. That's a savings of 20% off the cover price! I understand that accepting the 2 free books and gifts places me under no obligation to buy anything. I can always return a shipment and cancel at any time. Even if I never buy another book from Steeple Hill, the two free books and gifts are mine to keep forever.

123 IDN EL5H 323 IDN ELQH

Name	(PLEASE PRINT)	
Address		Apt. #
City	State/Prov.	Zip/Postal Code

Signature (if under 18, a parent or guardian must sign)

Order online at www.LoveInspiredSuspense.com

Or mail to Steeple Hill Reader Service™:

IN U.S.A.: P.O. Box 1867, Buffalo, NY 14240-1867
IN CANADA: P.O. Box 609, Fort Erie, Ontario L2A 5X3

Not valid to current Love Inspired Suspense subscribers.

Want to try two free books from another series?
Call 1-800-873-8635 or visit www.morefreebooks.com

* Terms and prices subject to change without notice. NY residents add applicable sales tax. Canadian residents will be charged applicable provincial taxes and GST. This offer is limited to one order per household. All orders subject to approval. Credit or debit balances in a customer's account(s) may be offset by any other outstanding balance owed by or to the customer. Please allow 4 to 6 weeks for delivery.

Your Privacy: Steeple Hill is committed to protecting your privacy. Our Privacy Policy is available online at www.eHarlequin.com or upon request from the Reader Service. From time to time we make our lists of customers available to reputable firms who may have a product or service of interest to you. If you would prefer we not share your name and address, please check here.

LISUS07

Love Inspired ®
SUSPENSE

TITLES AVAILABLE NEXT MONTH
Don't miss these four stories in May

VANISHED by Margaret Daley

When detective J. T. Logan's daughter is kidnapped, FBI agent Madison Spencer was brought in to help him find her. Madison's heart ached for the widowed father. All she could do was hope—and pray—for them all.

DEADLY PAYOFF by Valerie Hansen
The Secrets of Stoneley

Delia Blanchard was still reeling from learning that the woman shot to death in the library was her aunt, _not_ her mother, when she got a second shock. Her former love Shaun Murphy had been hired to repair her house. Was this their second chance?

DANGEROUS GAME by Lyn Cote
Harbor Intrigue

Returning home after spending time in prison, Grey Lawson was horrified to discover a new series of accidents that eerily mirrored his past. Deputy Trish Franklin had to tread carefully as she got involved with Grey, and he could only pray she wouldn't suffer for his sins.

CAUGHT IN THE ACT by Gayle Roper

Who would want to kill ordinary guy Arnie Meister? Reporter Merry Kramer was on the trail of the killer when she uncovered more murder suspects than she ever thought possible...and danger wasn't far behind.

LISCNM0407